"A girl like you and a guy like me!"

Becky could ask what Drew meant by a girl like her, but she already knew that he thought she was small-town and naive and hopelessly out of her depth, and not just in the ocean, either. What she wanted to know was what the last half of that sentence meant.

"What do you mean a guy like you?" she asked. Her voice was husky from the salt and from something else. Desire. Desire was burning like a white-hot coal in her belly. It was brand-new, it was embarrassing and it was wonderful.

"Look, Becky, I'm the kind of guy your mother used to warn you about."

"The kind who would jump in the water without a thought for his own safety to save someone else?"

"Not that kind!"

"What kind of guy, then?" she asked, gently curious.

"Self-centered. Here for a good time. Commitment-phobic. Good-time Charlie. Confirmed bachelor. They write whole articles about guys like me in your bridal magazines. And not about how to catch me, either. How to give a guy like me a wide berth."

He glanced at her. She bit her lip and his gaze rested there, hot with memory, until he made himself look away.

"It was just a kiss," she said, spirited in the posting of the bar...

"You're in shock," he...

If she was, she hoped it would never go away again, and soon!

Dear Reader,

My first book, *That Man From Texas* (using the pen name Quinn Wilder), came out in 1985. This year marks the thirtieth anniversary of my writing career. It has been an amazing ride, and I am so grateful to each of you who has been with me on this journey. Your notes, your letters, your messages, have been overwhelmingly loving and encouraging. Some highlights: a teacher in Russia used my books to teach English to her students. She said these little love stories had given her "hope to live." A survivor of Katrina let me know that after a year without laughter, it was one of my books that made her smile. A few years ago, at a conference in Seattle, a woman approached me and said she had read in the newspaper I would be there. She pulled a book out of a bag and asked, with endearing shyness, if I would sign it, that it was her most treasured possession. That book was *Dare to Dream*, my first novel as Cara Colter. My career has been wonderful and I am grateful for every moment of it and for you. Thank you!

With love,

Cara Colter

The Wedding Planner's Big Day

Cara Colter

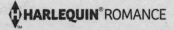
HARLEQUIN® ROMANCE

Recycling programs
for this product may
not exist in your area.

ISBN-13: 978-0-373-74381-0

The Wedding Planner's Big Day

First North American Publication 2016

Copyright © 2016 by Cara Colter

HARLEQUIN®

™ www.Harlequin.com

Printed in U.S.A.

Cara Colter shares her life in beautiful British Columbia, Canada, with her husband, nine horses and one small Pomeranian with a large attitude. She loves to hear from readers, and you can learn more about her and contact her through Facebook.

Books by Cara Colter

Harlequin Romance

The Vineyards of Calanetti

Soldier, Hero...Husband?

The Gingerbread Girls

Snowflakes and Silver Linings

The Cop, the Puppy and Me
Battle for the Soldier's Heart
Snowed in at the Ranch
Second Chance with the Rebel
How to Melt a Frozen Heart
Rescued by the Millionaire
The Millionaire's Homecoming
Interview with a Tycoon
Meet Me Under the Mistletoe
The Pregnancy Secret
Housekeeper Under the Mistletoe

Visit the Author Profile page
at Harlequin.com for more titles.

To all those readers who have made the past thirty years such an incredible journey.

CHAPTER ONE

"No."

A paper fluttered down on her temporary desk, slowly floating past Becky English's sun-burned nose. She looked up, and tried not to let her reaction to what she saw—or rather, whom she saw—show on her face.

The rich and utterly sexy timbre of the voice should have prepared her, but it hadn't. The man was gorgeous. Bristling with bad humor, but gorgeous, nonetheless.

He stood at least six feet tall, and his casual dress, a dark green sports shirt and pressed sand-colored shorts, showed off a beautifully made male body. He had the rugged look of a man who spent a great deal of time out of doors. There was no sunburn on his perfectly shaped nose!

He had a deep chest, a flat stomach and the narrow hips of a gunslinger. His limbs, relaxed, were sleekly muscled and hinted at easy strength.

The stranger's face was mesmerizing. His hair, dark brown and curling, touched the collar of his shirt. His eyes were as blue as the Caribbean Sea that Becky could just glimpse out the open patio door over the incredible broadness of his shoulder.

Unlike that sea, his eyes did not look warm and inviting. In fact, there was that hint of a gunslinger, again, something cool and formidable in his uncompromising gaze. The look in his eyes did not detract, not in the least, from the fact that his features were astoundingly perfect.

"And no," he said.

Another piece of paper drifted down onto her desk, this one landing on the keyboard of her laptop.

"And to this one?" he said. "Especially no."

And then a final sheet glided down, hit the lip of the desk, forcing her to grab it before it slid to the floor.

Becky stared at him, rather than the paper in her hand. A bead of sweat trickled down from his temple and followed the line of his face, slowly, slowly, slowly down to the slope of a perfect jaw, where he swiped at it impatiently.

It was hot here on the small, privately owned Caribbean island of Sainte Simone. Becky resisted a temptation to swipe at her own sweaty brow with the back of her arm.

She found her voice. "Excuse me? And you are?"

He raised an arrogant eyebrow at her, which made her rush to answer for him.

"You must be one of Allie's Hollywood friends," Becky decided.

It seemed to her that only people in Allie's field of work, acting on the big screen, achieved the physical beauty and perfection of the man in front of her. Only they seemed to be able to carry off that rather unsettling I-own-the-earth confidence that mere mortals had no hope of achieving. Besides, it was more than evident how the camera would love the gorgeous planes of his face, the line of his nose, the fullness of his lips...

"Are you?" she asked.

This was exactly why she had needed a guest list, but no, Allie had been adamant about that. She was looking after the guest list herself, and she did not want a single soul—up to and including her event planner, apparently—knowing the names of all the famous people who would be attending her wedding.

The man before Becky actually snorted in disgust, which was no kind of answer. Snorted. How could that possibly sound sexy?

"Of course, you are very early," Becky told him, trying for a stern note. Why was her heart beating like that, as if she had just run a sprint? "The wedding isn't for two weeks."

It was probably exactly what she should be expecting. People with too much money and too much time on their hands were just going to start showing up on Sainte Simone whenever they pleased.

"I'm Drew Jordan."

She must have looked as blank as she felt.

"The head carpenter for this circus."

Drew. Jordan. Of course! How could she not have registered that? She was actually expecting him. He was the brother of Joe, the groom.

Well, he might be the head carpenter, but she was the ringmaster, and she was going to have to establish that fact, and fast.

"Please do not refer to Allie Ambrosia's wedding as a circus," the ringmaster said sternly. Becky was under strict orders word of the wedding was not to get out. She was not even sure that was possible, with two hundred guests, but if it did get out, she did not want it being referred to as a circus by the hired help. The paparazzi would pounce on that little morsel of insider information just a little too gleefully.

There was that utterly sexy snort again.

"It is," she continued, just as sternly, "going to be the event of the century."

She was quoting the bride-to-be, Hollywood's latest "it" girl, Allie Ambrosia. She tried not to show that she, Becky English, small-town nobody, was just a little intimidated that she had been chosen to pull off that event of the century.

She now remembered Allie warning her about this very man who stood in front of her.

Allie had said, *My future brother-in-law is going to head up construction. He's a bit of a stick-in-the-mud. He's a few years older than Joe, but he acts, like, seventy-five. I find him quite cranky. He's the bear-with-the-sore-bottom type. Which explains why* he *isn't married.*

So, this was the future brother-in-law, standing in front of Becky, looking nothing at all like a stick-in-the-mud, or like a seventy-five-year-old. The bear-with-the-sore-bottom part was debatable.

With all those facts in hand, why was the one that stood out the fact that Drew Jordan was not married? And why would Becky care about that, at all?

Becky had learned there was an unexpected perk of being a wedding planner. She had named her company, with a touch of whimsy and a whole lot of wistfulness, Happily-Ever-After. However, her career choice had quickly killed what shreds of her romantic illusions had remained after the bitter end to her long engagement. She would be the first to admit she'd had far too many fairy-tale fantasies way back when she had been very young and hopelessly naive.

Flustered—here was a man who made a woman want to believe, all over again, in happy endings—but certainly not wanting to show it, Becky picked up the last paper Drew Jordan had cast down in front of her, the *especially no* one.

It was her own handiwork that had been cast so dismissively in front of her. Her careful, if somewhat rudimentary, drawing had a big black X right through the whole thing.

"But this is the pavilion!" she said. "Where are we supposed to seat two hundred guests for dinner?"

"The location is fine."

Was she supposed to thank him for that? Somehow words, even sarcastic ones, were lost to her. She sputtered ineffectually.

"You can still have dinner at the same place, on the front lawn in front of this monstrosity. Just no pavilion."

"This monstrosity is a castle," Becky said firmly. Okay, she, too, had thought when she had first stepped off the private plane that had whisked her here that the medieval stone structure looked strangely out of place amidst the palms and tropical flowers. But over the past few days, it had been growing on her. The thick walls kept it deliciously cool inside and every room she had peeked in had the luxurious feel of a five-star hotel.

Besides, the monstrosity was big enough to host two hundred guests for the weeklong extravaganza that Allie wanted for her wedding, and monstrosities like that were very hard, indeed, to find.

With the exception of an on-site carpenter, the island getaway came completely staffed with people who were accustomed to hosting remarkable events. The owner was record mogul Bart Lung, and many a musical extravaganza had been held here. The very famous fund-raising documentary *We Are the Globe*, with its huge cast of musical royalty, had been completely filmed and recorded here.

But apparently all those people had eaten in the very expansive castle dining room, which Allie had said with a sniff would not do. She had her heart set on alfresco for her wedding feast.

"Are you saying you can't build me a pavilion?" Becky tried for an intimidating, you-can-be-replaced tone of voice.

"Not can't. Won't. You have two weeks to get ready for the circus, not two years."

He was not the least intimidated by her, and she suspected it was not just because he was the groom's brother. She suspected it would take a great deal to intimidate Drew Jordan. He had that don't-mess-with-me look about his eyes, a set to his admittedly sexy mouth that said he was far more accustomed to giving orders than to taking them.

She debated asking him, again, not to call it a circus, but that went right along with not being able to intimidate him. Becky could tell by the stubborn set of his jaw that she might as well save her breath. She decided levelheaded reason would win the day.

"It's a temporary structure," she explained, the epitome of calm, "and it's imperative. What if we get inclement weather that day?"

Drew tilted his head at her and studied her for long enough that it was disconcerting.

"What?" she demanded.

"I'm trying to figure out if you're part of her Cinderella group or not."

Becky lifted her chin. Okay, so she wasn't Hollywood gorgeous like Allie was, and today—sweaty, casual and sporting a sunburned nose—might not be her best day ever, but why would it be debatable whether she was part of Allie's Cinderella group or not?

She didn't even know what that was. Why did she want to belong to it, or at least seem as if she could?

"What's a Cinderella group?" she asked.

"Total disconnect from reality," he said, nodding at the plan in her hand. "You can't build a pavilion that seats two hundred on an island where supplies have to be barged in. Not in two weeks, probably not even in two years."

"It's temporary," she protested. "It's creating an illusion, like a movie set."

"You're not one of her group," he decided firmly, even though Becky had just clearly demonstrated her expertise about movie sets.

"How do you know?"

"Imperative," he said. *"Inclement."* His lips twitched, and she was aware it was her use of the language that both amused him and told him she was not part of Allie's regular set. Really? She should not be relieved that it was vocabulary and not her looks that had set her apart from Allie's gang.

"Anyway, *inclement* weather—"

Was he making fun of her?

"—is highly unlikely. I Googled it."

She glanced at her laptop screen, which was already open on Google.

"This side of this island gets three days of rain per year," he told her. "In the last forty-two years of record-keeping, would you care to guess how often it has rained on the Big Day, June the third?"

The way he said *Big Day* was in no way preferable to *circus*.

Becky glared at him to make it look as if she was annoyed that he had beat her to the facts. She drew her computer to her, as if she had no intention of taking his word for it, as if she needed to check the details of the June third weather report herself.

Her fingers, acting entirely on their own volition, without any kind of approval from her mind, typed in D-r-e-w J-o-r-d-a-n.

CHAPTER TWO

DREW REGARDED BECKY ENGLISH thoughtfully. He had expected a high-powered and sophisticated West Coast event specialist. Instead, the woman before him, with her sunburned nose and pulled-back hair, barely looked as if she was legal age.

In fact, she looked like an athletic teenager getting ready to go to practice with the high school cheer squad. Since she so obviously was not the image of the professional woman he'd expected, his first impression had been that she must be a young Hollywood hanger-on, being rewarded for loyalty to Allie Ambrosia with a job she was probably not qualified to do.

But no, the woman in front of him had nothing of slick Hollywood about her. The vocabulary threw his initial assessment. The way she talked—with the earnestness of a student preparing for the Scripps National Spelling Bee—

made him think that the bookworm geeky girl had been crossed with the high school cheerleader. Who would have expected that to be such an intriguing combination?

Becky's hair was a sandy shade of brown that looked virgin, as if it had never been touched by dye or blond highlights. It looked as if she had spent about thirty seconds on it this morning, scraping it back from her face and capturing it in an elastic band. It was a rather nondescript shade of brown, yet so glossy with good health, Drew felt a startling desire to touch it.

Her eyes were plain old brown, without a drop of makeup around them to make them appear larger, or wider, or darker, or greener. Her skin was pale, which would have been considered unfashionable in the land of endless summer that he came from. Even after only a few days in the tropics, most of which he suspected had been spent inside, the tip of her nose and her cheeks were glowing pink, and she was showing signs of freckling. There was a bit of a sunburn on her slender shoulders.

Her teeth were a touch crooked, one of the front ones ever so slightly overlapping the other one. It was oddly endearing. He couldn't help but notice, as men do, that she was as flat as a board.

Drew Jordan's developments were mostly in Los Angeles. People there—especially people who could afford to buy in his subdivisions—were about the furthest thing from *real* that he could think of.

The women he dealt with had the tiny noses and fat lips, the fake tans and the unwrinkled foreheads. They had every shade of blond hair and the astonishingly inflated breast lines. Their eyes were widened into a look of surgically induced perpetual surprise and their teeth were so white you needed sunglasses on to protect you from smiles.

Drew was not sure when he had become used to it all, but suddenly it seemed very evident to him why he had. There was something about all that fakeness that was *safe* to a dyed-in-the-wool bachelor such as himself.

The cheerleader bookworm girl behind the desk radiated something that was oddly threatening. In a world that seemed to celebrate phony everything, she seemed as if she was 100 percent real.

She was wearing a plain white tank top, and if he leaned forward just a little bit he could see cutoff shorts. Peeking out from under the desk was a pair of sneakers with startling pink laces in them.

"How did you get mixed up with Allie?" he asked. "You do not look the way I would expect a high-profile Hollywood event planner to look."

"How would you expect one to look?" she countered, insulted.

"Not, um, wholesome."

She frowned.

"Take it as a compliment," he suggested.

She looked uncertain about that, but marshaled herself.

"I've run a very successful event planning company for several years," she said with a proud toss of her head.

"In Los Angeles," he said with flat disbelief.

"Well, no, not exactly."

He waited.

She looked flustered, which he enjoyed way more than he should have. She glared at him. "My company serves Moose Run and the surrounding areas."

Was she kidding? It sounded like a name Hollywood would invent to conjure visions of a quaintly rural and charming America that hardly existed anymore. But, no, she had that cute and geeky earnestness about her.

Still, he had to ask. "Moose Run? Seriously?"

"Look it up on Google," she snapped.

"Where is it? The mountains of Appalachia?"

"I said look it up on Google."

But when he crossed his arms over his chest and raised an eyebrow at her, she caved.

"Michigan," she said tersely. "It's a farm community in Michigan. It has a population of about fourteen thousand. Of course, my company serves the surrounding areas, as well."

"Ah. Of course."

"Don't say *ah* like that!"

"Like what?" he said, genuinely baffled.

"Like *that explains everything.*"

"It does. It explains everything about you."

"It does not explain everything about me!" she said. "In fact, it says very little about me."

There were little pink spots appearing on her cheeks, above the sunburned spots.

"Okay," he said, and put up his hands in mock surrender. Really, he should have left it there. He should keep it all business, let her know what she could and couldn't do construction wise with severe time restraints, and that was it. His job done.

But Drew was enjoying flustering her, and the little pink spots on her cheeks.

"How old are you?" he asked.

She folded her arms over her own chest—battle stations—and squinted at him. "That is an inappropriate question. How old are you?" she snapped back.

"I'm thirty-one," he said easily. "I only asked because you look sixteen, but not even Allie would be ridiculous enough to hire a sixteen-year-old to put together this cir—event—would she?"

"I'm twenty-three and Allie is not ridiculous!"

"She isn't?"

His brother's future wife had managed to arrange her very busy schedule—she was shooting a movie in Spain—to grant Drew an audience, once, on a brief return to LA, shortly after Joe had phoned and told him with shy and breathless excitement he was getting married.

Drew had not been happy about the announcement. His brother was twenty-one. To date, Joe hadn't made many major decisions without consulting Drew, though Drew had been opposed to the movie-set building and Joe had gone ahead anyway.

And look where that had led. Because, in

a hushed tone of complete reverence, Joe had told Drew *who* he was marrying.

Drew's unhappiness had deepened. He had shared it with Joe. His normally easygoing, amenable brother had yelled at him.

Quit trying to control me. Can't you just be happy for me?

And then Joe, who was usually happy-go-lucky and sunny in nature, had hung up on him. Their conversations since then had been brief and clipped.

Drew had agreed to meet Joe here and help with a few construction projects for the wedding, but he had a secret agenda. He needed to spend time with his brother. Face-to-face time. If he managed to talk some sense into him, all the better.

"I don't suppose Joe is here yet?" he asked Becky with elaborate casualness.

"No." She consulted a thick agenda book. "I have him arriving tomorrow morning, first thing. And Allie arriving the day of the wedding."

Perfect. If he could get Joe away from Allie's influence, his mission—to stop the wedding, or at least reschedule it until cooler heads prevailed—seemed to have a better chance of succeeding.

Drew liked to think he could read people—the woman in front of him being a case in point. But he had come away from his meeting with Allie Ambrosia feeling a disconcerting sense of not being able to read her at all.

Where's my brother? Drew had demanded.

Allie Ambrosia had blinked at him. *No need to make it sound like a kidnapping.*

Which, of course, was exactly what Drew had been feeling it was, and that Allie Ambrosia was solely responsible for the new Joe, who could hang up on his brother and then ignore all his attempts to get in touch with him.

"Allie Ambrosia is sensitive and brilliant and sweet."

Drew watched Becky with interest as the blaze of color deepened over her sunburn. She was going to rise to defend someone she perceived as the underdog, and that told him almost as much about her as the fact that she hailed from Moose Run, Michigan.

Drew was just not sure who would think of Allie Ambrosia as the underdog. He may have been frustrated about his inability to read his future sister-in-law, but neither *sensitive* nor *sweet* would have made his short list of descriptive adjectives. Though they probably would have for Becky, even after such a short acquaintance.

Allie? Brilliant, maybe. Though if she was it had not shown in her vocabulary. Still, he'd been aware of the possibility of great cunning. She had seemed to Drew to be able to play whatever role she wanted, the real person, whoever and whatever that was, hidden behind eyes so astonishingly emerald he'd wondered if she enhanced the color with contact lenses.

He'd come away from Allie frustrated. He had agreed to build some things for the damn wedding, hoping, he supposed, that this seeming capitulation to his brother's plans would open the door to communication between them and he could talk some sense into Joe.

He'd have his chance tomorrow. Today, he could unabashedly probe the secrets of the woman his brother had decided to marry.

"And you would know Allie is sensitive and brilliant and sweet, why?" he asked Becky, trying not to let on just how pleased he was to have found someone who actually seemed to know Allie.

"We went to school together."

Better still. Someone who knew Allie *before* she'd caught her big break playing Peggy in a sleeper of a movie called *Apple Mountain*.

"Allie Ambrosia grew up in Moose Run, Michigan?" He prodded her along. "That is not in the official biography."

He thought Becky was going to clam up, careful about saying anything about her boss and old school chum, but her need to defend won out.

"Her Moose Run memories may not be her fondest ones," Becky offered, a bit reluctantly.

"I must say Allie has come a long way from Moose Run," he said.

"How do you know? How well do you know Allie?"

"I admit I'm assuming, since I hardly know her at all," Drew said. "This is what I know. She's had a whirlwind relationship with my little brother, who is building a set on one of her movies. They've known each other weeks, not months. And suddenly they are getting married. It can't last, and this is an awful lot of money and time and trouble to go to for something that can't last."

"You're cynical," she said, as if that was a bad thing.

"We can't all come from Moose Run, Michigan."

She squinted at him, not rising to defend herself, but staying focused on him, which made him very uncomfortable. "You are really upset that they are getting married."

He wasn't sure he liked that amount of perception. He didn't say anything.

"Actually, I think you don't like weddings, period."

"What is this, a party trick? You can read my mind?" He intended it to sound funny, but he could hear a certain amount of defensiveness in his tone.

"So, it's true then."

"Big deal. Lots of men don't like weddings."

"Why is that?"

He frowned at her. He wanted to ferret out some facts about Allie, or talk about construction. He was comfortable talking about construction, even on an ill-conceived project like this. He was a problem solver. He was not comfortable discussing feelings, which an aversion to weddings came dangerously close to.

"They just don't like them," he said stubbornly. "Okay, I don't like them."

"I'm curious about who made you your brother's keeper," she said. "Shouldn't your parents be talking to him about this?"

"Our parents are dead."

When something softened in her face, he deliberately hardened himself against it.

"Oh," Becky said quietly, "I'm so sorry. So you, as older brother, are concerned, and at the same time have volunteered to help out. That's very sweet."

"Let's get something straight right now. There is nothing sweet about me."

"So why did you agree to help at all?"

He shrugged. "Brothers help each other."

Joe's really upset by your reaction to our wedding, Allie had told him. *If you agreed to head up the construction, he would see it was just an initial reaction of surprise and that of course you want what is best for your own brother.*

Oh, he wanted what was best for Joe, all right. Something must have flashed across Drew's face, because Becky's brow lowered.

"Are you going to try to stop the wedding?" she asked suspiciously.

Had he telegraphed his intention to Allie, as well? "Joe's all grown up, and capable of making up his own mind. But so am I. And it seems like a crazy, impulsive decision he's made."

"You didn't answer the question."

"You'd think he would have asked me what I thought," Drew offered grimly.

A certain measure of pain escaped in that

statement, and so he frowned at Becky, daring her to give him sympathy.

Thankfully, she did not even try. "Is this why I can't have the pavilion? Are you trying to sabotage the whole thing?"

"No," he said curtly. "I'll do what I can to give my brother and his beloved a perfect day. If he comes to his senses before then—" He lifted a shoulder.

"If he changes his mind, that would be a great deal of time and money down the tubes," Becky said.

Drew lifted his shoulder again. "I'm sure you would still get paid."

"That's hardly the point!"

"It's the whole point of running a business." He glanced at her and sighed. "Please don't tell me you do it for love."

Love.

Except for what he felt for his brother, his world was comfortably devoid of that pesky emotion. He was sorry he'd even mentioned the word in front of Becky English.

CHAPTER THREE

"SINCE YOU BROUGHT it up," Becky said solemnly, "I got the impression from Allie that she and your brother are head over heels in love with one another."

"Humph." There was no question his brother was over the moon, way past the point where he could be counted on to make a rational decision. Allie was more difficult to interpret. Allie was an actress. She pretended for a living. It seemed to Drew his brother's odds of getting hurt were pretty good.

"Joe could have done worse," Becky said, quietly. "She's a beautiful, successful woman."

"Yeah, there's that."

"There's that cynicism again."

Cynical. Yes, that described Drew Jordan to an absolute T. And he liked being around people who were as hard-edged as him. Didn't he?

"Look, my brother is twenty-one years old.

That's a little young to be making this kind of decision."

"You know, despite your barely contained scorn for Moose Run, Michigan, it's a traditional place where they love nothing more than a wedding. I've planned dozens of them."

Drew had to bite his tongue to keep from crushing her with a sarcastic *Dozens?*

"I've been around this for a while," she continued. "Take it from me. Age is no guarantee of whether a marriage is going to work out."

"He's known her about eight weeks, as far as I can tell!" He was confiding his doubts to a complete stranger, which was not like him. It was even more unlike him to be hoping this wet-behind-the-ears country girl from Moose Run, Michigan, might be able to shed some light on his brother's mysterious, flawed decision-making process. This was why he liked being around people as *not* sweet as himself. There was no probing of the secrets of life.

"That doesn't seem to reflect on how the marriage is going to work out, either."

"Well, what does then?"

"When I figure it out, I'm going to bottle it and sell it," she said. There was that earnestness again. "But I've planned the weddings of lots of young people who are still together.

Young people have big dreams and lots of energy. You need that to buy your first house and have your first baby, and juggle three jobs and—"

"Baby?" Drew said, horrified. "Is she pregnant?" That would explain his brother's rush to the altar of love.

"I don't think so," Becky said.

"But you don't know for certain."

"It's none of my business. Or yours. But even if she is, lots of those kinds of marriages make it, too. I've planned weddings for people who have known each other for weeks, and weddings for people who have known each other for years. I planned one wedding for a couple who had lived together for sixteen years. They were getting a divorce six months later. But I've seen lots of marriages that work."

"And how long has your business been running?"

"Two years," she said.

For some reason, Drew was careful not to be quite as sarcastic as he wanted to be. "So, you've seen lots that work for two years. Two years is hardly a testament to a solid relationship."

"You can tell," she said stubbornly. "Some people are going to be in love forever."

Her tone sounded faintly wistful. Something uncomfortable shivered along his spine. He had a feeling he was looking at one of those forever kinds of girls. The kind who were not safe to be around at all.

Though it would take more than a sweet girl from Moose Run to penetrate the armor around his hard heart. He felt impatient with himself for the direction of his thoughts. Wasn't it proof that she was already penetrating something since they were having this discussion that had nothing to do with her unrealistic building plans?

Drew shook off the feeling and fixed Becky with a particularly hard look.

"Sheesh, maybe you are a member of the Cinderella club, after all."

"Despite the fact I run a company called Happily-Ever-After—"

He closed his eyes. "That's as bad as Moose Run."

"It is a great name for an event planning company."

"I think I'm getting a headache."

"But despite my company name, I have long since given up on fairy tales."

He opened his eyes and looked at her. "Uh-huh," he said, loading those two syllables with doubt.

"I have!"

"Lady, even before I heard the name of your company, I could tell that you have 'I'm waiting for my prince to come' written all over you."

"I do not."

"You've had a heartbreak."

"I haven't," she said. She was a terrible liar.

"Maybe it wasn't quite a heartbreak. A romantic disappointment."

"Now who is playing the mind reader?"

"Aha! I was right, then."

She glared at him.

"You'll get over it. And then you'll be in the prince market all over again."

"I won't."

"I'm not him, by the way."

"Not who?"

"Your prince."

"Of all the audacious, egotistical, ridiculous—"

"Just saying. I'm not anybody's prince."

"You know what? It is more than evident you could not be mistaken for Prince Charming even if you had a crown on your head and tights and golden slippers!"

Now that he'd established some boundaries, he felt he could tease her just a little. "Please tell me you don't like men who wear tights."

"What kind of man I like is none of your business!"

"Correct. It's just that we will be working in close proximity. My shirt has been known to come off. It has been known to make women swoon." He smiled.

He was enjoying this way more than he had a right to, but it was having the desired effect, putting up a nice big wall between them, and he hadn't even had to barge in the construction material to do it.

"I'm not just *getting* a headache," she said. "I've had one since you marched through my door."

"Oh, great," he said. "There's nothing I like as much as a little competition. Let's see who can give who a bigger headache."

"The only way I could give you a bigger headache than the one you are giving me is if I smashed this lamp over your head."

Her hand actually came to rest on a rather heavy-looking brass lamp on the corner of her desk. It was evident to him that she would have loved to do just that if she wasn't such a prim-and-proper type.

"I'm bringing out the worst in you," he said with satisfaction. She looked at her hand, resting on the lamp, and looked so appalled with herself that Drew did the thing he least wanted to do. He laughed.

Becky snatched her hand back from the brass lamp, annoyed with herself, miffed that she was providing amusement for the very cocky Mr. Drew Jordan. She was not the type who smashed people over the head with lamps. Previously, she had not even been the type who would have ever thought about such a thing. She had dealt with some of the world's—or at least Michigan's—worst Bridezillas, and never once had she laid hand to lamp. It was one of the things she prided herself in. She kept her cool.

But Drew Jordan had that look of a man who could turn a girl inside out before she even knew what had hit her. He could make a woman who trusted her cool suddenly aware that fingers of heat were licking away inside her, begging for release. And it was disturbing that he knew it!

He was laughing at her. It was super annoying that instead of being properly indignant, steeling herself against attractions that he was as aware of as she was, she could not help but notice how cute he was when he laughed—that sternness stripped from his face, an almost boyish mischievousness lurking underneath.

She frowned at her computer screen, pretending she was getting down to business and that she had called up the weather to double-check his facts. Instead, she learned her head of construction was also the head of a multi-million-dollar Los Angeles development company.

The bride's future brother-in-law was not an out-of-work tradesman that Becky could threaten to fire. He ran a huge development company in California. No wonder he seemed to be impatient at being pressed into the service of his very famous soon-to-be sister-in-law.

No wonder he'd been professional enough to Google the weather. Becky wondered why she hadn't thought of doing that. It was nearly the first thing she did for every event.

It was probably because she was being snowed under by Allie's never-ending requests. Just now she was trying to find a way to honor Allie's casually thrown-out email, received that morning, which requested freshly planted lavender tulips—picture attached—to line the outdoor aisle she would walk down toward her husband-to-be.

Google, that knowledge reservoir of all things, told Becky she could not have lavender tulips—or any kind of tulip for that matter—in the tropics in June.

What Google confirmed for her now was not the upcoming weather forecast or the impossibility of lavender tulips, but that Drew Jordan was used to million-dollar budgets.

Becky, on the other hand, had started shaking when she had opened the promised deposit check from Allie. Up until then, it had seemed to her that maybe she was being made the butt of a joke. But that check—made out to Happily-Ever-After—had been for more money than she had ever seen in her life.

With trembling fingers she had dialed the private cell number Allie had provided.

"Is this the budget?"

"No, silly, just the deposit."

"What exactly is your budget?" Becky had asked. Her voice had been shaking as badly as her fingers.

"Limitless," Allie had said casually. "And I fully intend to exceed it. You don't think I'm going to be outdone by Roland Strump's daughter, do you?"

"Allie, maybe you should hire whoever did the Strump wedding, I—"

"Nonsense. Have fun with it, for Pete's sake. Haven't you ever had fun? I hope you and Drew don't manage to bring down the mood of the whole wedding. Sourpusses."

Sourpuss? She was studious to be sure, but sour? Becky had put down the phone contemplating that. Had she ever had fun? Even at Happily-Ever-After, planning fun events for other people was very serious business, indeed.

Well, now she knew who Drew was. And Allie had been right when it came to him. He could definitely be a sourpuss! It was more worrying that he planned to take off his shirt. She had to get back to business.

"Mr. Jordan—"

"Drew is fine. And what should I call you?"

Barnum. "Becky is fine. We can't just throw a bunch of tables out on the front lawn as if this were the church picnic."

"We're back to that headache." His lips twitched. "I'm afraid my experience with church picnics has been limited."

Yes, it was evident he was all devilish charm and dark seduction, while it was written all over her that that was what she came from: church picnics and 4-H clubs, a place where the Fourth of July fireworks were *the* event of the year.

She shifted her attention to the second *no*. "And we absolutely need some sort of dance floor. Have you ever tried to dance on grass? Or sand?"

"I'm afraid," Drew said, "that falls outside of the realm of my experience, too. And you?"

"Oh, you know," she said. "We like to dust up our heels after the church picnic."

He nodded, as if that was more than evident to him and he had missed her sarcasm completely.

She focused on his third veto. She looked at her clumsy drawing of a small gazebo on the beach. She had envisioned Allie and Joe saying their vows under it, while their guests sat in beautiful lightweight chairs looking at them and the sea beyond them.

"And what's your complaint with this one?"

"I'll forgive you this oversight because of where you are from."

"Oversight?"

"I wouldn't really expect a girl from Michigan to have foreseen this. The *wedding*—" he managed to fill that single word with a great deal of contempt "—according to my notes, is supposed to take place at 4:00 p.m. on June third."

"Correct."

"If you Google the tide chart for that day, you'll see that your gazebo would have water lapping up to the third stair. I'm not really given to omens, but I would probably see that as one."

She was feeling very tired of Google, except in the context of learning about him. It seemed to her he was the kind of man who brought out the weakness in a woman, even one who had been made as cynical as she had been. Because she felt she could ogle him all day long. And he knew it, she reminded herself.

"So," she said, a little more sharply than intended, "what do you suggest?"

"If we scratch the pavilion for two hundred—"

"I can get more people to help you."

He went on as if she hadn't spoken. "I can probably build you a rudimentary gazebo at a different location."

"What about the dance floor?"

"I'll think about it."

He said that as if he were the boss, not her. From what she had glimpsed about him on the internet he was very used to being in charge.

And he obviously knew his stuff, and was good with details. He had spotted the weather and the tides, after all. Really, she should be grateful. What if her bride had marched down her tulip-lined aisle—or whatever the aisle ended up being lined with—to a wedding gazebo that was slowly being swallowed by water?

It bothered her to even think it, but Drew Jordan was right. That would have been a terrible omen.

Still, gratitude was not what Becky felt. Not at all.

"You are winning the headache contest by a country mile," she told him.

"I'm no kind of expert on the country," he said, without regret, "but I am competitive."

"What did Allie tell you? Are you in charge of construction?"

"Absolutely."

He said it too quickly and with that self-assured smile of a man way too used to having his own way, particularly with the opposite sex.

"I'm going to have to call Allie and see what that means," Becky said, steeling herself against that smile. "I'm happy to leave construction to you, but I think I should have the final word on what we are putting up and where."

"I'm okay with that. As long as it's reasonable."

"I'm sure we define that differently."

He flashed his teeth at her again. "I'm sure we do."

"Would it help you do your job if I brought more people on-site? Carpenters and such?"

"That's a great idea, but I don't work with strangers. Joe and I have worked together a lot. He'll be here tomorrow."

"That wouldn't be very romantic, him building the stuff for his own wedding."

"Or you could see it as him putting an investment and some effort into his own wedding."

She sighed. "You want him here so you can try to bully him out of getting married."

"I resent the implication I would bully him."

But Becky was stunned to see doubt flash across those self-confident features. "He isn't talking to you, is he?" Becky guessed softly.

She could tell Drew was not accustomed to this level of perception. He didn't like it one little bit.

"I have one of my teams arriving soon. And Joe. I'm here a day early to do some initial assessments. What I need is for you to pick the site for the exchange of vows so that I can put together a plan. We don't have as much time as you think."

Which was truly frightening, because she did not think they had any time at all. Becky looked at her desk: flowers to be ordered, ceremony details to be finalized, accommodations to be organized, boat schedules, food, not just for the wedding feast, but for the week to follow, and enough staff to pull off pampering two hundred people.

"And don't forget fireworks," she added.

"Excuse me?"

"Nothing," she muttered. She did not want to be thinking of fireworks around a man like Drew Jordan. Her eyes drifted to his lips. If she were ever to kiss someone like that, it would be the proverbial fireworks. And he knew it, too. That was why he was smiling evilly at her!

Suddenly, it felt like nothing in the world would be better than to get outside away from this desk—and from him—and see this beautiful island. So far, she had mostly experienced it by looking out her office window. The sun would be going down soon. She could find a place to hold the wedding and watch the sun go down.

"Okay," she said. "I'll find a new site. I'll let you know as soon as I've got it."

"Let's do it together. That might save us some grief."

She was not sure that doing anything with him was going to save her some grief. She needed to get away from him…and the thoughts of fireworks he had caused.

CHAPTER FOUR

"I'D PREFER TO do it on my own," Becky said, even though it seemed ungracious to say so. She felt a need to establish who was running the cir—show.

"But here's the problem," Drew said with annoying and elaborate patience.

"Yes?"

"You'll pick a site on your own, and then I'll go look at it and say no, and so then you'll pick another site on your own, and I'll go look at it and say no."

She scowled at him. "You're being unnecessarily negative."

He shrugged. "I'm just making the point that we could, potentially, go on like that endlessly, and there is a bit of a time crunch here."

"I think you just like using the word *no*," she said grumpily.

"Yes," he said, deadpan, as if he was not being deliberately argumentative now.

She should argue that she was quite capable of picking the site by herself and that she had no doubt her next selection would be fine, but her first choice was not exactly proof of that. And besides, then who would be the argumentative one?

"It's too late today," Drew decided. "Joe's coming in on the first flight. Why don't we pick him up and the three of us will pick a site that works for the gazebo?"

"Yes, that would be fine," she said, aware her voice was snapping with ill grace. Really, it was an opportunity. Tomorrow morning she would not scrape her hair back into a careless ponytail. She would apply makeup to hide how her fair skin, fresh out of a Michigan winter, was already blotchy from the sun.

Should she wear her meet-the-potential-client suit, a cream-colored linen by a famous designer? That would certainly make a better impression than shorty-shorts and a sleeveless tank that could be mistaken for underwear!

But the following morning it was already hot, and there was no dry cleaner on the island to take a sweat-drenched dress to.

Aware she was putting way too much effort into her appearance, Becky donned white shorts and a sleeveless sun-yellow shirt. She put on makeup and left her hair down. And then she headed out of her room.

She met Drew on the staircase.

He looked unreasonably gorgeous!

"Good morning," she said. She was stupidly pleased by how his eyes trailed to her hair and her faintly glossed lips.

He returned her greeting gruffly and then went down the stairs in front of her, taking them two at a time. But he stopped and held open the main door for her. They were hit by a wall of heat.

"It's going to be even hotter in two weeks," Drew told her, when he watched her pause and draw in her breath on the top stair of the castle.

"Must you be so negative?"

"Pragmatic," he insisted. "Plus…"

"Don't tell me. I already know. You looked it up. That's how you know it will be even hotter in two weeks."

He nodded, pleased with himself.

"Keep it up," she warned him, "and you'll have to present me with the prize. A king-size bottle of headache relief."

They stood at the main door to the castle, huge half circles of granite forming a staircase down to a sparkling expanse of emerald lawn.

The lawn was edged with a row of beautifully swaying palm trees, and beyond that was a crescent of powdery white sand beach.

"That beach looks so much less magical now that I know it's going to be underwater at four o'clock on June the third."

Drew glanced at Becky. She looked older and more sophisticated with her hair down and makeup on. She had gone from cute to attractive.

It occurred to Drew that Becky was the kind of woman who brought out things in a man that he would prefer to think he didn't have. Around a woman like this a man could find himself wanting to protect himself—and her—from disappointments. That's all he wanted for Joe, too, not to bully him but to protect him.

He'd hated that question, the one he hadn't answered. Had he bullied his brother? He hoped not. But the sad truth was Joe had been seven when Drew, seventeen, was appointed his guardian. Drew had floundered, in way over his head, and he'd resorted to doing whatever needed to be done to get his little brother through childhood.

No wonder his brother was so hungry for

love that he'd marry the first beautiful woman who blinked sideways at him.

Unless he could talk some sense into him. He cocked his head. He was pretty sure he could hear the plane coming.

"How hot is it supposed to be on June third?" she asked. He could hear the reluctance to even ask in her voice.

"You know that expression? Hotter than Hades—"

"Never mind. I get it. All the more reason that we really need the pavilion," she said. "We'll need protection from the sun. I planned to have the tables running this way, so everyone could just turn their heads and see the ocean as the sun is going down. The head table could be there, at the bottom of the stairs. Imagine the bride and groom coming down that staircase to join their guests."

Her voice had become quite dreamy. Had she really tried to tell him she was not a romantic? He knew he'd pegged it. She'd had some kind of setback in the romance department, but inside her was still a giddy girl with unrealistic dreams about her prince coming. He had to make sure she knew that was not him.

"Well, I already told you, you can't have that," he said gruffly. He did not enjoy puncturing her dream as much as he wanted to. He did not enjoy being mean as much as he would have liked. He told himself it was for her own good.

He was good at doing things for other people's own good. You could ask Joe, though his clumsy attempts at parenting were no doubt part of why his brother was running off half-cocked to get married.

"I'm sure we can figure out something," Becky said of her pavilion dream.

"We? No, *we* can't."

This was better. They were going to talk about practicalities, as dream-puncturing as those could be!

The plane was circling now, and they moved toward the airstrip.

He continued, "What you're talking about is an open, expansive structure with huge unsupported spans. You'd need an architect and an engineer."

"I have a tent company I use at home," Becky said sadly, "but they are booked nearly a year in advance. I've tried a few others. Same story. Plus, the planes that can land here aren't big enough to carry that much canvas, and you have to book the supply barge. There's only one with a flat enough bottom to dock here.

An unlimited budget can't get you what you might think."

"Unlimited?" He heard the horror in his voice.

She ignored him. "Are you sure I'd need an architect and an engineer, even for something so temporary?"

He slid her a look. She looked quite deflated by all this.

"Especially for something so temporary," he told her. "I'm sure the last thing Allie wants is to be making the news for the collapse of her wedding pavilion. I can almost see the headlines now. 'Three dead, one hundred and eighty-seven injured, event planner and building contractor missing.'"

He heard her little gasp and glanced at her. She was blushing profusely.

"Not missing like *that*," he said.

"Like what?" she choked.

"Like whatever thought is making you blush like that."

"I'm not blushing. The sun has this effect on me."

"Sheesh," he said, as if she had not denied the blush at all. "It's not as if I said that while catastrophe unfolded all around them, the event planner and the contractor went missing *together*."

"I said I wasn't blushing! I never would have thought about us together in any way." Her blush deepened.

He watched her. "You aren't quite the actress that your employer is."

"I am not thinking of us together," she insisted. Her voice was just a little shrill. He realized he quite enjoyed teasing her.

"No?" he said, silkily. "You and I seeking shelter under a palm frond while disaster unfolds all around us?"

Her eyes moved skittishly to his lips and then away. He took advantage of her looking away to study her lips in profile. They were plump little plums, ripe for picking. He was almost sorry he had started this. Almost.

"You're right. You are not a prince. You are evil," she decided, looking back at him. There was a bit of reluctant laughter lurking in her eyes.

He twirled an imaginary moustache. "Yes, I am. Just waiting for an innocent from Moose Run, Michigan, to cross my path so that in the event of a tropical storm, and a building collapse, I will still be entertained."

A little smile tugged at the lips he had just

noticed were quite luscious. He was playing a dangerous game.

"Seriously," she said, and he had a feeling she was the type who did not indulge in light-hearted banter for long, "Allie doesn't want any of this making the news. I'm sure she told you the whole wedding is top secret. She does not want helicopters buzzing her special day."

Drew felt a bit cynical about that. Anyone who wanted a top secret wedding did not invite two hundred people to it. Still, he decided, now might not be the best time to tell Becky a helicopter buzzing might be the least of her worries. When he'd left the States yesterday, all the entertainment shows had been buzzing with the rumors of Allie's engagement.

Was the famous actress using his brother—and everyone else, including small-town Becky English—to ensure Allie Ambrosia was front and center in the news just as her new movie was coming out?

Even though it went somewhat against his blunt nature, the thought that Becky might be being played made Drew soften his bad news a bit. "This close to the equator it's fully dark by six o'clock. The chance of heatstroke for your two hundred guests should be minimized by that."

They took a path through some dense vegetation. On the other side was the airstrip.

"Great," she said testily, though she was obviously relieved they were going to discuss benign things like the weather. "Maybe I can create a kind of 'room' feeling if I circle the area with torches and dress up the tables with linens and candles and flowers and hope for the best."

"Um, about the torches? And candles?" He squinted at the plane touching down on the runway.

"What?"

"According to Google, the trade winds seem to pick up in the late afternoon. And early evening. Without any kind of structure to protect from the wind, I think they'll just blow out. Or worse."

"So, first you tell me I can't have a structure, and then you tell me all the problems I can expect because I don't have a structure?"

He shrugged. "One thing does tend to lead to another."

"If the wind is strong enough to blow out the candles, we could have other problems with it, too."

"Oh, yeah, absolutely. Tablecloths flying off tables. Women's dresses blowing up over their heads. Napkins catching fire. Flower arrangements being smashed. There's really a whole lot of things people should think about before planning their wedding on a remote island in the tropics."

Becky glared at him. "You know what? I barely know you and I hate you already."

He nodded. "I have that effect on a lot of people."

He watched the plane taxi toward them and grind to a halt in front of them.

"I'm sure you do," she said snippily.

"Does this mean our date under the palm frond is off?"

"It was never on!"

"You should think about it—the building collapsed, the tablecloths on fire, women's dresses blowing over their heads as they run shrieking…"

"Please stop."

But he couldn't. He could tell he very nearly had her where he wanted her. Why did he feel so driven to make little Miss Becky English angry? But also to make her laugh?

"And you and me under a palm frond, licking wedding cake off each other's fingers."

At first she looked appalled. But then a smile tickled her lips. And then she giggled.

And then she was laughing. In a split second, every single thing about her seemed transformed. She went from plain to pretty.

Very pretty.

This was exactly what he had wanted: to glimpse what the cool Miss English would look like if she let go of control.

It was more dangerous than Drew had anticipated. It made him want to take it a step further, to make her laugh harder or to take those little lips underneath his and...

He reminded himself she was not the type of girl he usually invited out to play. Despite the fact she was being relied on to put on a very sophisticated event, there didn't seem to be any sophistication about her.

He had already figured out there was a heartbreak in her past. That was the only reason a girl as apple pie as her claimed to be jaundiced about romance. He could tell it wasn't just dealing with people's wedding insanity that had made her want to be cynical, even as it was all too evident she was not. He had seen the truth in the dreamy look when she had started talking about how she wanted it all to go.

He could tell by looking at her exactly what

she needed, and it wasn't a job putting together other people's fantasies.

It was a husband who adored her. And three children. And a little house where she could sew curtains for the windows and tuck bright annuals into the flower beds every year.

It was whatever the perfect life in Moose Run, Michigan, looked like.

Drew knew he could never give her those things. Never. He'd experienced too much loss and too much responsibility in his life.

Still, there was one thing a guy as jaundiced as him did not want or need. To be stuck on a deserted island with a female whose laughter could turn her from a plain old garden-variety girl next door into a goddess in the blink of an eye.

He turned from her quickly and watched as the door of the plane opened. The crew got off, opened the cargo hold and began unloading stuff beside the runway.

He frowned. No Joe.

He took his phone out of his pocket and stabbed in a text message. He pushed Send, but the island did not have great service in all places. The message to his brother did not go through.

Becky was searching his face, which he carefully schooled not to show his disappointment.

"I guess we'll have to find that spot ourselves. Joe will probably come on the afternoon flight. Let's see what we can find this way."

Instead of following the lawn to where it dropped down to the beach, he followed it north to a line of palm trees. A nice wide trail dipped into them, and he took it.

"It's like jungle in here," she said.

"Think of the possibilities. Joe could swing down from a vine. In a loincloth. Allie could be waiting for him in a tree house, right here."

"No, no and especially no," she said.

He glanced behind him. She had stopped to look at a bright red hibiscus. She plucked it off and tucked it behind her ear.

"In the tropics," he told her, "when you wear a flower behind your ear like that, it means you are available. You wouldn't want the cook getting the wrong idea."

She glared at him, plucked the flower out and put it behind her other ear.

"Now it means you're married."

"There's no winning, is there?" she asked lightly.

No, there wasn't. The flower looked very

exotic in her hair. It made him very aware, again, of the enchantment of tropical islands. He turned quickly from her and made his way down the path.

After about five minutes in the deep shade of the jungle, they came out to another beach. It was exposed to the wind, which played in the petals of the flower above her ear, lifted her bangs from her face and pressed her shirt to her.

"Oh," she called, "it's beautiful."

She had to shout because unlike the beach the castle overlooked, this one was not in a protected cove.

It was a beautiful beach. A surfer would probably love it, but it would have to be a good surfer. There were rocky outcrops stretching into the water that looked like they would be painful to hit and hard to avoid.

"It's too loud," he said over the crashing of the waves. "They'd be shouting their vows."

He turned and went back into the shaded jungle. For some reason, he thought she would just follow him, and it took him a few minutes to realize he was alone.

He turned and looked. The delectable Miss Becky English was nowhere to be seen. He went back along the path, annoyed. Hadn't he made it perfectly clear they had time constraints?

When he got back out to the beach, his heart went into his throat. She had climbed up onto one of the rocky outcrops. She was standing there, bright as the sun in that yellow shirt, as a wave smashed on the rock just beneath her. Her hands were held out and her face lifted to the spray of white foam it created. With the flower in her hair, she looked more like a goddess than ever, performing some ritual to the sea.

Did she know nothing of the ocean? Of course she didn't. They had already established that. That, coming from Moose Run, there were things she could not know about.

"Get down from there," he shouted. "Becky, get down right now."

He could see the second wave building, bigger than the first that had hit the rock. The waves would come in sets. And the last wave in the set would be the biggest.

The wind swallowed his voice, though she turned and looked at him. She smiled and waved. He could see the surf rising behind her alarmingly. The second wave hit the rock. She turned away from him, and hugged herself in delight as the spray fell like thick mist all around her.

"Get away from there," he shouted. She turned and gave him a puzzled look. He started to run.

Becky had her back to the third wave when it hit. It hit the backs of her legs. Drew saw her mouth form a surprised O, and then her arms were flailing as she tried to regain her balance. The wave began pulling back, with at least as much force as it had come in with. It yanked her off the rock as if she were a rag doll.

CHAPTER FIVE

BECKY FELT THE shocked helplessness as her feet were jerked out from under her and she was swept off the rock. The water closed over her head and filled her mouth and nose. She popped back up like a cork, but her swimming skills were rudimentary, and she was not sure they would have helped her against the fury of the sea. She was being pulled out into what seemed to be an endless abyss. She tried frantically to swim back in toward shore. In seconds she was as exhausted as she had ever been.

I'm going to drown, she thought, stunned, choking on water and fear. How had this happened? One moment life had seemed so pleasant and beautiful and then…it was over.

Her life was going to be over. She waited, helplessly, for it to flash before her eyes. Instead, she found herself thinking that Drew had been right. It hadn't been a heartbreak. It had been a romantic disappointment. Ridiculous to think that right now, but on the other hand, right now seemed as good a time as any to be acutely and sadly aware of things she had missed.

"Hey!" His voice carried over the crashing of the sea. "Hang on."

Becky caught a glimpse of the rock she had fallen off. Drew was up there. And then she went under the water again.

When she surfaced, Drew was in the water, slashing through the roll of the waves toward her. "Don't panic," he called over the roar of the water pounding the rock outcropping.

She wanted to tell him it was too late for that. She was already panicked.

"Tread," he yelled. "Don't try to swim. Not yet. Look at my face. Nowhere else. Look at me."

Her eyes fastened on his face. There was strength and calm in his features, as if he did this every day. He was close to her now.

"I'm going to come to you," he shouted, "but you have to be calm first. If you panic, you will kill us both."

It seemed his words, and the utter strength and determination in his face, poured a honey of calm over her, despite the fact she was still bobbing like a cork in a ravaged sea. He seemed to see or sense the moment she stopped panicking, and he moved in close.

She nearly sobbed with relief when Drew reached out and touched her, then folded his arms around her and pulled her in tight to him. He was strong in the water—she suspected, abstractly, he was strong everywhere in his life—and she rested into his embrace, surrendering to his warmth. She could feel the power of him in his arms and where she was pressed into the wet slickness of his chest.

"Just let it carry you," he said. "Don't fight it anymore"

It seemed as if he could be talking about way more than water. It could be a message about life.

It seemed the water carried them out forever, but eventually it dumped them in a calmer place, just beyond where the waves began to crest. Becky could feel the water lose its grip on her, even as he refused to.

She never took her eyes off his face. Her mind seemed to grow calmer and calmer, even amused. If this was the last thing she would see, it told her, that wasn't so bad.

"Okay," he said, "can you swim?"

"Dog paddle." The water was not cold, but her voice was shaking.

"That will do. Swim that way. Do your best. I've got you if you get tired." He released her.

That way was not directly to the shore. He was asking her to swim parallel to the shore instead of in. But she tried to do as he asked. She was soon floundering, so tired she could not lift her arms.

"Roll over on your back," he said, and she did so willingly. His hand cupped her chin and she was being pulled through the water. He was an enormously strong swimmer.

"Okay, this is a good spot." He released her again and she came upright and treaded water. "Go toward shore. I've got you, I'm right with you."

She was scared to go back into the waves. It was too much. She was exhausted. But she glanced at his face once more and found her own courage there.

"Get on your tummy, flat as a board, watch for the next wave and ride it in. Watch for those rocks on the side."

She did as she was told. She knew she had no choice. She had to trust him completely. She felt the wave lift her up and drive her toward the shore at a stunning speed. And then it spit her out. She was lying in shallow water, but she could already feel the wave pulling at her, trying to drag her back in. She used what little strength she had left to scramble to her knees and crawl through the sugar pebbles of the sand.

Drew came and scooped her out of the water, lifted her to his chest and struggled out of the surf.

On the beach, above the foaming line of the ocean, he set her down on her back in the sun-warmed sand. For a moment she looked at the clear and endless blue of the sky. It was the very same sky it had been twenty minutes ago, but everything felt changed, some awareness sharp as glass within her. She rolled over onto her stomach and rested her head on her fore-arms. He flung himself onto the sand beside her, breathing hard.

"Did you just save my life?" she whispered. Her voice was hoarse. Her throat hurt from swallowing salt water. She felt drowsy and ex-traordinarily peaceful.

"You'll want to make sure this beach is posted before guests start arriving," he finally said, when he spoke.

"You didn't answer the question," she said,

taking a peek at him over her folded arm. "Is that a habit with you?"

Drew didn't answer. She looked at him, feeling as if she was drinking him in, as if she could never get enough of looking at him. It was probably natural to feel that way after someone had just saved your life, and she did not try to make herself stop.

She was in a state of altered awareness. She could see the water beading on his eyelashes, and the sun streaming through his wet hair. She could see through his soaked shirt where it was plastered to his body.

"Did you just save my life?" she asked again.

"I think you Michigan girls should stay away from the ocean."

"Do you ever just answer a question, Drew Jordan? Did you save my life?"

He was silent again.

"You did," she finally answered for him.

She could not believe the gratitude she felt. To be alive. It was as if the life force was zinging inside her, making her every cell quiver.

"You risked yourself for me. I'm nearly a complete stranger."

"No, you're not. Winning the headache competition, by the way."

"By a country mile?"

"Oh, yeah."

"That was incredibly heroic." She was not going let him brush it off, though he was determined to.

"Don't make it something it wasn't. I'm nobody's hero."

Just like he had insisted earlier he was nobody's prince.

"Well," she insisted, "you're mine."

He snorted, that sexy, cynical sound he made that was all his own and she found, right now, lying here in the sand, alive, so aware of herself and him, that she liked that sound very much, despite herself.

"I've been around the ocean my whole life," he told her grimly. "I grew up surfing some pretty rough water. I knew what I was doing. Unlike you. That was incredibly stupid."

In her altered state, she was aware that he thought he could break the bond that had been cementing itself into place between them since the moment he had entered the water to rescue her.

"Life can change in a blink," he said sternly. "It can be over in a blink."

He was lecturing her. She suddenly *needed* him to know she could not let him brush it off like that. She needed him to know that the life force was flowing through her. She had an incredible sense of being alive.

"You were right," she said, softly.

There was that snort again. "Of course I'm right. You don't go climbing up on rocks when the surf is that high."

"Not about that. I mean, okay, about that, too, but I wasn't talking about that."

"What were you talking about?"

"It wasn't a heartbreak," Becky said. "It was a romantic disappointment."

"Huh?"

"That's what I thought of when I went into the water. I thought my whole life would flash before my eyes, but instead I thought of Jerry."

"Look, you're obviously in shock and we need to—"

"He was my high school sweetheart. We'd been together since I was seventeen. I'd always assumed we were going to get married. Everybody in the whole town thought we would get married. They called us Salt and Pepper."

"You know what? This will keep. I have to—"

"It won't keep. It's important. I have to say it before I forget it. Before this moment passes."

"Oh, sheesh," he said, his tone indicating he wanted nothing more than for this moment to pass.

"I wanted that. I wanted to be Salt and Pepper, *forever.* My parents had split up the year before. It was awful. My dad owned a hardware store. One of his clerks. And him."

"Look, Becky, you are obviously rattled. You don't have to tell me this."

She could no more have stopped herself from telling him than she could have stopped those waves from pounding on the shore.

"They had a baby together. Suddenly, they were the family we had always been. That we were supposed to be. It was horrible, seeing them all over town, looking at each other. Pushing a baby carriage. I wanted it back. I wanted that feeling of being part of something back. Of belonging."

"Aw, Becky," he said softly. "That sucks. Really it does, but—"

But she had to tell all of it, was compelled to. "Jerry went away to school. My mom didn't have the money for college, and it seemed my dad had new priorities.

"I could see what the community needed, so I started my event company."

"Happily-Ever-After," he said. "Even though you had plenty of evidence of the exact opposite."

"It was way more successful than I had

thought it could be. It was way more successful than Jerry thought it could be, too. The more successful I became, the less he liked me."

"Okay. Well. Some guys are like that."

"He broke up with me."

"Yeah, sorry, but now is not the time—"

"This is the reason it's important for me to say it right now. I understand something I didn't understand before. I thought my heart was broken. It is a terrible thing to suffer the humiliation of being ditched in a small town. It was a double humiliation for me. First my dad, and then this. But out there in the water, I felt glad. I felt if I had married him, I would have missed something. Something essential."

"Okay, um—"

"A grand passion."

He said a word under his breath that they disapproved of in Moose Run, Michigan.

"Salt and pepper?" She did a pretty good imitation of his snort. "Why settle for boring old salt and pepper when the world is full of so many glorious flavors?"

"Look, I think you've had a pretty bad shake-up. I don't have a clue what you are talking about, so—"

She knew she was making Drew Jordan wildly uncomfortable, but she didn't care. She planned to make him more uncomfortable yet. She leaned toward him. He stopped talking and watched her warily.

She needed to know if the life force was as intense in him right now as it was in her. She needed to take advantage of this second chance to be alive, to really live.

She touched Drew's back through the wetness of his shirt, and felt the sinewy strength there. The strength that had saved her.

She leaned closer yet. She touched her forehead to his, as if she could make him *feel* what was going on inside her, since words could not express it. He had a chance to move away from her. He did not. He was as caught in what was unfolding as she had been in the wave.

And then, she touched her lips to his, delicately, *needing* the connection to intensify.

His lips tasted of salt and strength and something more powerful and more timeless than the ocean. That desire that people had within them, not just to live, but to go on.

For a moment, Drew was clearly stunned to find her lips on his. But then, he seemed to get whatever she was trying to tell him, in this primal language that seemed the only thing that could express the celebration of all that lived within her.

His lips answered hers. His tongue chased the ridges of her teeth, and then probed, gently, ever so gently...

It was Becky's turn to be stunned. It was everything she had hoped for. It was everything she had missed.

No, it was *more* than what she had hoped for, and more than what she could have ever imagined. A kiss was not simply a brushing of lips. No! It was a journey, it was a ride on pure energy, it was a connection, it was a discovery, it was an intertwining of the deepest parts of two people, of their souls.

Drew stopped kissing her with such abruptness that she felt forlorn, like a blanket had been jerked from her on a freezing night. He said Moose Run's most disapproved-of word again.

She *liked* the way he said that word, all naughty and nasty.

He found his feet and leaped up, staring down at her. He raked a hand through his hair, and water droplets scattered off his crumpled hair, sparkling like diamonds in the tropical heat. His shirt, crusted in golden sand, was clinging to his chest.

"Geez," he said. "What was that about?"

"I don't know," she said honestly. *But I liked it.*

"A girl like you does not kiss a guy like me!"

She could ask what he meant by a girl like her, but she already knew that he thought she was small town and naive and hopelessly out of her depth, and not just in the ocean, either. What she wanted to know was what the last half of that sentence meant.

"What do you mean a guy like you?" she asked. Her voice was husky from the salt and from something else. Desire. Desire was burning like a white-hot coal in her belly. It was brand-new, it was embarrassing and it was wonderful.

"Look, Becky, I'm the kind of guy your mother used to warn you about."

Woo-hoo, she thought, but she didn't dare say it. Instead, she said, "The kind who would jump in the water without a thought for his own safety to save someone else?"

"Not that kind!"

She could point out to him that he obviously *was* that kind, and that the facts spoke for themselves, but she probed the deeper part of what was going on.

"What kind of guy then?" she asked, gently curious.

"Self-centered. Commitment-phobic. Good-time Charlie. Confirmed bachelor. They write whole articles about guys like me in your bridal magazines. And not about how to catch me, either. How to give a guy like me a wide berth."

"Just in case you didn't listen to your mother's warnings," she clarified.

He glanced at her. She bit her lip and his gaze rested there, hot with memory, until he seemed to make himself look away.

"I wouldn't have pictured you as any kind of expert about the content of bridal magazines," she said.

"That is not the point!"

"It was just a kiss," she pointed out mildly, "not a posting of the banns."

"You're in shock," he said.

If she was, she hoped she could experience it again, and soon!

CHAPTER SIX

DREW LOOKED AT Becky English. Sprawled out, belly down in the sand, she looked like a drowned rat, her hair plastered to her head, her yellow shirt plastered to her lithe body, both her shirt and her white shorts transparent in their wetness. For a drowned rat, and for a girl from Moose Run, Michigan, she had on surprisingly sexy underwear.

She looked like a drowned rat, and she was a small-town girl, but she sure as hell did not kiss like either one of those things. There had been nothing sweet or shy about that kiss!

It had been hungry enough to devour him.

But, Drew told himself sternly, she was exceedingly vulnerable. She was obviously stunned from what had just happened to her out there at the mercy of the ocean. It was possible she had banged her head riding that final wave in. The blow might have removed the filter from her brain that let her know what was, and what wasn't, appropriate.

But good grief, that kiss. He had to make sure nothing like that ever happened again! How was he going to be able to look at her without recalling the sweet, salty taste of her mouth? Without recalling the sweet welcome? Without recalling the flash of passion, the pull of which was at least as powerful as those waves?

"Becky," he said sternly, "don't make me your hero. I've been cast in that role before, and I stunk at it."

Drew had been seventeen when he became a parent to his brother. He had a sense of having grown up too fast and with too heavy a load. He was not interested in getting himself back into a situation where he was responsible for someone else's happiness and well-being. He didn't feel the evidence showed he had been that good at it.

"It was just a kiss," she said again, a bit too dreamily.

It wasn't just a kiss. If it had been just a kiss he would feel nothing, the same as he always did when he had just a kiss. He wouldn't be feeling this need to set her straight.

"When were you cast in that role before?

How come you stank at it?" she asked softly. He noticed that, impossibly, the flower had survived in her hair. Its bright red petals were drooping sadly, kissing the tender flesh of her temple.

"This is not the time or the place," he said curtly before, in this weakened moment, in this contrived atmosphere of closeness, he threw himself down beside her, and let her save him, the way he had just saved her.

"Are you hurt?" he asked, cold and clinical. "Any bumps or bruises? Did you hit your head?"

Thankfully, she was distracted, and considered his question with an almost comical furrowing of her brow.

"I don't think I hit my head, but my leg hurts," she decided. "I think I scraped it on a rock coming in."

She rolled onto her back and then struggled to sit up. He peered over her shoulder. There was six inches of scrapes on the inside of her thigh, one of the marks looked quite deep and there was blood clumping in the sand that clung to it.

What was wrong with him? The first thing he should have done was check for injuries.

He stripped off his wet shirt and got down

beside her. This was what was wrong with him. He was way too aware of her. The scent of the sea was clinging to her body, a body he was way too familiar with after having dragged her from the ocean and then accepted the invitation of her lips.

Becky was right. There was something exhilarating about snatching life back out of the jaws of death. That's why he was so aware of her on every level, not thinking with his customary pragmatism.

He brushed the sand away from her wound. He should have known touching the inner thigh of a girl like Becky English was going to be nothing like a man might have expected.

"Ow," she said, and her fingers dug into his shoulder and then lingered there. "Oh, my," she breathed. "You did warn me what would happen if you took your shirt off."

"I was kidding," he said tersely.

"No, you weren't. You were warning me off."

"How's that working for you, Drew?" he muttered to himself. He cleaned the sand away from her wound as best he could, then wrapped it in his soaked shirt.

She sighed with satisfaction like the geeky

girl who had just gotten all the words right at the spelling bee. "Women adore you."

"Not ones as smart as you," he said. "Can you stand? We have to find a first aid kit. I think that's just a superficial scrape, but it's bleeding quite a lot and we need to get it looked after."

He helped her to her feet, still way too aware, steeling himself against the silky resilience of her skin. She swayed against him. Her wet curves were pressed into him, and her chin was pressed sharply into his chest as she looked up at him with huge, unblinking eyes.

Had he thought, just an hour ago, her eyes were ordinary brown? They weren't. They were like melted milk chocolate, deep and rich and inviting.

"You were right." She giggled. "I'm swooning."

"Let's hope it's not from blood loss. Can you walk?"

"Of course."

She didn't move.

He sighed and scooped her up, cradling her to his chest, one arm under her knees, the other across her back. She was lighter than he could have believed, and her softness pressed into him was making him way more vulnerable than the embraces of women he'd known who had far more in the curvy department.

"You're very masterful," she said, snuggling into him.

"In this day and age how can that be a good thing?"

"It's a secret longing."

He did not want to hear about her secret longings!

"If you don't believe me, read—"

"Stop it," he said grimly.

"I owe you my life."

"I said stop it."

"You are not the boss over me."

"That's what I was afraid of."

He carried her back along the path. She was small and light and it took no effort at all. At the castle, he found the kitchen, an enormous room that looked like the kind of well-appointed facility one would expect to find in a five-star hotel.

"Have you got a first aid attendant here?" Drew asked one of the kitchen staff, who went and fetched the chef.

The chef showed him through to an office adjoining the kitchen, and Drew settled Becky in a chair. The chef sent in a young man with a first aid kit. He was slender and golden-skinned with dark, dark hair and almond-shaped eyes that matched.

"I am Tandu," he said. "I am the medical man." His accent made it sound as if he had said *medicine man*.

Relived that he could back off from more physical contact with the delectable Miss Becky, Drew motioned to where she sat.

Tandu set down his first aid kit and crouched down in front of her. He carefully unwrapped Drew's wet shirt from her leg. He stared at Becky's injury for a moment, scrambled to his feet, picked up the first aid kit and thrust it at Drew.

"I do not do blood."

"What kind of first aid attendant doesn't—?"

But Tandu had already fled.

Drew, even more aware of her now that he had nearly escaped, went and found a pan of warm water, and then cleaned and dressed her wound, steeling himself to be as professional as possible.

Becky stared down at the dark head of the man kneeling at her feet. He pressed a warm, wet cloth against the tender skin of her inner thigh, and she gasped at the sensation that jolted through her like an electric shock.

He glanced up at her, then looked back to his task quickly. "Sorry," he muttered. "I will try to make this as painless as possible."

Despite the fact his touch was incredibly tender—or maybe because of it—it was one of the most deliciously painful experiences of Becky's life. He carefully cleaned the scrapes, dabbed an ointment on them and then wound clean gauze around her leg.

She could feel a quiver within her building. There was going to be an earthquake if he didn't finish soon! She longed to reach out and touch his hair, to brush the salt and sand from it. She reached out.

A pan dropped in the kitchen, and she felt reality crashing back in around her. She snatched her hand back, just as Drew glanced up.

"Are you okay?"

"Sure," she said shakily, but she really wasn't. What she felt like was a girl who had been very drunk, and who had done all kinds of uninhibited and crazy things, and was now coming to her senses.

She had kissed Drew Jordan shamelessly. She had shared all her secrets with him. She had blabbered that he was masterful, as if she enjoyed such a thing! Now she had nearly touched his hair, as if they were lovers instead of near strangers!

Okay, his hand upon her thigh was obviously creating confusion in the more primal cortexes of her brain, but she had to pull herself together.

"There," he said, rocking back on his heels and studying the bandage around her thigh, "I think—"

She didn't let him finish. She shot to her feet, gazed down at her bandaged thigh instead of at him. "Yes, yes, perfect," she said. She sounded like a German engineer approving a mechanical drawing. Her thigh was tingling unmercifully, and she was pretty sure it was from his touch and not from the injury.

"I have to get to work," she said in a strangled voice.

He stood up. "You aren't going to work. You're going to rest for the afternoon."

"But I can't. I—"

"I'm telling you, you need to rest."

She thought, again, of telling him he was masterful. Good grief, she could feel the blush rising up her cheeks. She had probably created a monster.

In him and in herself.

"Go to bed," he said. Drew's voice was as

caressing as his hand had been, and just as seductive. "Just for what is left of the afternoon. You'll be glad you did."

You did not discuss bed with a man like this! And especially not after he had just performed intimate rituals on your thigh! Particularly not after you had noticed his voice was seduction itself, all deep and warm and caressing.

You did not discuss bed with a man like this once you had come to your senses. She opened her mouth to tell him she would decide for herself what needed to be done. It would not involve the word *bed*. But before she could speak, he did.

"I'll go scout a spot for the wedding. Joe will be here in a while. By the time you wake up, we'll have it all taken care of."

All her resolve to take back the reins of her own life dissolved, instantly, like sugar into hot tea.

It felt as if she was going to start crying. When was the last time anything had been taken care of for her? After her father had left, her poor shattered mother had absconded on parenting. It felt as if Becky had been the one who looked after everything. Jerry had seemed to like her devoting herself to organizing his life. Even her career took advantage of the fact that Becky English was the one who looked after things, who tried valiantly to fix all and to achieve perfection. She took it all on…until the weight of it nearly crushed her.

Where had that thought come from? She *loved* her job. Putting together joyous and memorable occasions for others had soothed the pain of her father's abandonment, and had, thankfully, been enough to fill her world ever since the defection of Jerry from her personal landscape.

Or had been enough until less than twenty-four hours ago, when Drew Jordan had showed up in her life and showed her there was still such a thing as a hero.

She turned and fled before she did something really foolish. Like kissing him again.

Becky found that as much as she would have liked to rebel against his advice, she had no choice but to take it. Clear of the kitchen, her limbs felt like jelly, heavy and nearly shaking with exhaustion and delayed reaction to all the unexpected adventures of the day. It took every bit of remaining energy she had to climb the stone staircase that led to the wing of the castle with her room in it.

She went into its cool sanctuary and peeled off her wet clothes. It felt like too much effort to even find something else to put on. She left the clothes in a heap and crept under the cool sheets of the welcoming bed. Within seconds she was fast asleep.

She dreamed that someone was knocking on her door, and when she went to answer it, Drew Jordan was on the other side of it, a smile of pure welcome on his face. He reached for her, he pulled her close, his mouth dropped over hers...

Becky started awake. She was not sure what time it was, though the light suggested early evening, which meant she had frittered away a whole precious afternoon sleeping.

She wanted to leap from bed, but her body would not let her. She felt, again, like the girl who had had too much to drink. She tested each of her limbs. It was official. Her whole body hurt. Her head hurt. Her mouth and throat felt raw and dry. But mostly, she felt deeply ashamed. She had lost control, and she hated that.

Her door squeaked open.

"How you doing?"

She shot up in bed, pulled the sheet more tightly around herself. "What are you doing here?"

"I knocked. When there was no answer, I

thought I'd better check on you. You slept a long time."

Drew Jordan looked just as he had in the dream—gorgeous. Though in real life there was no expression of tender welcome on his face. It did not look like he was thinking about sweeping her into his big strong arms.

In fact, he slipped into the room, but rested himself against the far wall—as far away from her as possible—those big, strong arms folded firmly across his chest. He was wearing a snowy-white T-shirt that showed off the sun-bronzed color of his arms, and khaki shorts that showed off the long, hard muscle of equally sun-bronzed legs.

"A long time?" She found her cell phone on the bedside table. "It's only five. That's not so bad."

"Um, maybe you should have a look at the date on there."

She frowned down at her phone. Her mouth fell open. "What? I slept an entire day? But I couldn't have! That's impossible."

She started to throw back the covers, then remembered she had slipped in between the sheets naked. She yanked them up around her chin.

"It was probably the best thing you could do. Your body knows what it needs."

She looked up at him. Her body, treacherous thing, did indeed know what it needed! And all of it involved him.

"If you would excuse me," she said, "I really need—"

Now her brain, treacherous thing, silently screamed *you*.

"Are you okay?"

No! It simply was not okay to be this aware of him, to yearn for his touch and his taste.

"I'm fine. Did your brother come?" she asked, desperate to distract him from her discomfort, and from the possibility of him discerning what was causing it.

"Nope. I can't seem to reach him on my phone, either."

"Oh, Drew," she said softly.

Her tone seemed to annoy him. "You don't really look fine," he decided.

"Okay, I'm not fine. I don't have time to sleep away a whole day. Despite all that rest, I feel as if I've been through the spin cycle of a giant washing machine. I hurt everywhere, worse than the worst hangover ever."

"You've had a hangover?" He said this with insulting incredulousness.

"Of course I have. Living in Moose Run

isn't like taking vows to become a nun, you know."

"You would be wasted as a nun," he said, and his gaze went to her lips before he looked sharply away.

"Let's talk about that," she said.

"About you being wasted as a nun?" he asked, looking back at her, surprised.

"About the fact you think you would know such a thing about me. I don't normally act like that. I would never, under ordinary circumstances, kiss a person the way I kissed you. Naturally, I'm mortified."

He lifted an eyebrow.

"There was no need to throw myself at you, no matter how grateful and discombobulated I was."

His lips twitched.

"It's not funny," she told him sternly. "It's embarrassing."

"It's not your wanton and very un-nun-like behavior I was smiling about."

"Wanton?" she squeaked.

"It was the fact you used *discombobulated* in a sentence. I can't say as I've ever heard that before."

"Wanton?" she squeaked again.

"Sorry. Wanton is probably overstating it."

"Probably?"

"We don't all have your gift for picking exactly the right word," he said. He lifted a shoulder. "People do weird things when they are in shock. Let's move past it, okay?"

Actually, she would have preferred to find out exactly what he meant by wanton—it had been a little kiss really, it didn't even merit the humiliation she was feeling about it—but she didn't want to look like she was unwilling to move past it.

"Okay," she said grudgingly. "Though just for the record, I want you to know I don't like masterful men. At all."

"No secret longing?"

He was teasing her! There was a residue of weakness in her, because she liked it, but it would be a mistake to let him know her weaknesses.

"As you have pointed out," Becky said coolly, "I was in shock. I said and did things that were completely alien to my nature. Now, let's move past it."

Something smoky happened to his eyes. His gaze stopped on her lips. She had the feeling he would dearly like to prove to her that some things were not as alien to her nature as she wanted them both to believe.

But he fended off the temptation, with apparent ease, pushing himself away from the wall and heading back for the door. "You have one less thing to worry about. I think I have the pavilion figured out."

"Really?" She would have leaped up and gave him a hug, except she was naked underneath the sheet, he already thought she was wanton enough, and she was not exposing anything to him, least of all not her longing to let other people look after things for a change. And to feel his embrace once more, his hard, hot muscles against her naked flesh.

"You do?" she squeaked, trying to find a place to put her gaze, anywhere but his hard, hot muscles.

"I thought about what you said, about creating an illusion. I started thinking about driving some posts, and suspending fabric from them. Something like a canopy bed."

She squinted at him. That urge to hold him, to feel him, to touch him, was there again, stronger. It was because he was looking after things, taking on a part of the burden without being asked. It was because he had listened to her.

Becky English, lying there in her bed, naked, with her sheet pulled up around her chin, studied her ceiling, so awfully aware that a woman could fall for a guy like him before she even knew what had happened to her.

CHAPTER SEVEN

THANKFULLY FOR BECKY, Drew Jordan had already warned her about guys like him.

"What does a confirmed bachelor know about canopy beds?" she said, keeping her gaze on the ceiling and her tone deliberately light. "No, never mind. I don't want to know. I think I'm still slightly discombobulated."

"Admit it."

She glanced over at him just as he grinned. His teeth were white and straight. He looked way too handsome. She returned her gaze to the ceiling. "I just did. I'm still slightly discombobulated."

"Not that! Admit it's brilliant."

She couldn't help but smile. And look at him again. "It is. It's brilliant. It will create that illusion of a room, and possibly provide some protection from the sun if we use fabric as a kind of ceiling. It has the potential to be exceedingly romantic, too. Which is why I'm surprised you came up with it."

"Hey, nobody is more surprised than me. Sadly, after traipsing all over the island this afternoon, I still haven't found a good site for the ceremony. But you might as well come see what's going on with the pavilion."

She should not appear too eager. But really? Pretending just felt like way too much effort. She would have to chalk it up to her near drowning and the other rattling events of the day. "Absolutely. Give me five minutes."

"Sure. I'll meet you on the front stairs."

Of course, it took Becky longer than five minutes. She had to shower off the remains of her adventure. She had sand in places she did not know sand could go. Her hair was destroyed. Her leg was a mess and she had to rewrap it after she was done. She had faint bruising appearing in the most unlikely places all over her body.

She put on her only pair of long pants—as uninspiring as they were in a lightweight grey tweed—and a long-sleeved shirt in a shade of hot pink that matched some of the flowers that bloomed in such abundance on this island. Her outfit covered the worst of the damage to her poor battered body, but there was nothing she could do about the emotional battering she was receiving. And it wasn't his fault. Drew Jordan was completely oblivious to the effect he was having on her.

Or accustomed to it!

Becky dabbed on a bit of makeup to try to hide the crescent moons from under her eyes. She looked exhausted. How was that possible after nearly twenty-four hours of sleep? At the last minute, she just touched a bit of gloss to her lips. It wasn't wrong to want him to look at them, but she hoped she would not be discombobulated enough to offer them to him again anytime in the near future.

"Or any future!" she told herself firmly.

She had pictured Drew waiting impatiently for her, but when she arrived at the front step, he had out a can of spray paint and was marking big X's on the grassy lawn in front of the castle.

Just when she was trying not to think of kisses anymore. What was this clumsy artwork on the lawn all about? An invitation? A declaration of love? A late Valentine?

"Marking where the posts should go," he told her, glancing toward her and then looking back at what he was doing. "Can you come stand right here and hold the tape measure?"

So much for a declaration of love! Good grief. She had always harbored this secret and very unrealistic side. She thought Jerry had cured her of her more fantastic romantic notions, but no, some were like little seeds inside her, waiting for the first hint of water and sun to sprout into full-fledged fairy tales. Being rescued from certain death by a very good-looking and extremely competent man who had so willingly put his own life on the line for her had obviously triggered her most fanciful longings.

She just needed to swat herself up the side of the head with the facts. She and Drew Jordan barely knew one another, and before she was swept off the rock they had been destined to butt heads.

She had to amend that: she barely knew Drew Jordan, but he knew her better than he should because she had blurted out her whole life story in a moment of terrible weakness. It was just more evidence that she must have hit her head somewhere in that debacle. Except for the fact she was useful for holding the tape measure, he hardly seemed aware that she was there.

Finally, he rolled up the tape measure. "What do you think?"

His X's formed a large rectangle. She could picture it already with a silken canopy and the posts swathed in fabric. She could picture the tables and the candles, and music and a beautiful bride and groom.

"I think it's going to be perfect," she breathed. And for the first time since she had taken on this job, she felt like maybe it would be.

How much of that had to do with the man who was, however reluctantly, helping her make it happen?

"Don't get your hopes up too high," he said. "Perfection is harder to achieve than you think. And we still have the evening tropical breezes to contend with. And I haven't found a ceremony site. It could go sideways yet."

"Especially if you talk to your brother?"

He rolled his shoulders. "There doesn't seem to be much chance of that happening. But there are a lot of things that could go sideways before the big day."

Yes, she had seen in recent history how quickly things could go sideways. In fact, when she looked at him, she was pretty sure Drew Jordan was the kind of man who could make your whole life go sideways with no effort on his part at all.

"Let's go see if we can find a place for the ceremony."

She *had* to go with him. It was her job. But tropical breezes seemed to be the least of her problems at the moment.

"I should be getting danger pay," she muttered to herself.

"Don't worry, I won't be letting you anywhere near any rocks."

No sense clarifying with him that was not where the danger she was worried about was coming from. Not at all.

They were almost at the edge of the lawn when a voice stopped them.

"Miss Becky. Mr. Drew."

They turned to see Tandu struggling across the lawn with a huge wicker basket. "So sorry, no good with blood. Take you to place for wedding vow now."

"Oh, did you tell him we were looking for a new ceremony site?" Becky asked. "That was smart."

"Naturally, I would like to take credit for being smart, but I didn't tell him. They must do weddings here all the time. He's used to this."

"Follow, follow," Tandu ordered.

They fell into step behind him, leaving the lawn and entering the deep, vibrant green of the jungle forest. Birds chattered and the breeze lifting huge leaves made a sound, too.

"Actually, the owner of the island told me they had hosted some huge events here, but never a wedding," Becky told Drew. "He's the music mogul, Bart Lung. He's a friend of Allie's. He's away on business but he'll be back for the wedding. He's very excited about it."

"Are you excited about meeting him?"

"I guess I hadn't really thought about it. We better catch up to Tandu, he's way ahead of us."

Drew contemplated what had just happened with a trace of self-loathing.

Are you excited about meeting him? As bad as asking the question was how much he had liked her answer. She genuinely seemed not to have given a thought to meeting Bart Lung.

But what had motivated Drew to ask such a question? Surely he hadn't been feeling a bit threatened about Becky meeting the famously single and fabulously wealthy record broker? He couldn't possibly have felt the faintest little prickle of…jealousy.

He never felt jealous. He'd had women he had dated who had tried to make him jealous, and he'd been annoyed by how juvenile that felt. But at the heart of it, he knew they had wanted him to show what he couldn't: that he cared.

But he'd known from the moment she had instigated that kiss that Becky English was different from what his brother liked to call the rotating door of women in his life. The chemistry between them had been unexpected, but Drew had had chemistry before. He wasn't sure exactly what it was about the cheerleader-turned-event-planner that intrigued him, but he knew he had to get away from it.

Which was exactly why he had marched up to her room. He had two reasons, and two reasons only, to interact with her: the pavilion and the ceremony site. He'd promised his brother and Becky his help, and once the planning for his assigned tasks was solidly in place, he could minimize his interactions with her. He was about to get very busy with construction. That would leave much less time for contemplating the lovely Miss English.

"I hate to say it," he told Becky, looking at Tandu's back disappearing down a twisting path in front of them, "but I've already been over this stretch of the island. There is no—"

"This way, please." Tandu had stopped and was holding back thick jungle fronds. "Path overgrown a bit. I will tell gardening staff. Important for all to be ready for big day, eh?"

It was just a short walk, and the path opened onto a beautiful crescent of beach. Drew studied it from a construction point of view. He could see the high tide line, and it would be perfect for building a small pavilion and setting up chairs for the two hundred guests. Three large palms grew out of the center of the beach, their huge leathery leaves shading almost the entire area.

Becky, he could see, was looking at it from a far less practical standpoint than he was. She turned to look at him. Her eyes were shiny with delight, and those little plump lips were curved upward in the nicest smile.

Task completed! Drew told himself sternly. Pavilion, check. Wedding location, check. Missing brother...well, that had nothing to do with her. He had to get away from her—and her plump little lips—and *stay* away from her.

"It's perfect," he said. "Do you agree?"

She turned those shining eyes to him. "Agree?" she said softly. "Have you ever seen such a magical place in your whole life?"

He looked around with magic in mind rather than construction. He was not much of a magic kind of person, but he supposed he had not seen a place quite like this before. The whole beach was ringed with thick shrubs with dark green foliage. Tucked in amongst the foliage was an abundance of pale yellow and white flowers the size of cantaloupes. The flowers seemed to be emitting a perfume that was sweet and spicy at the same time. Unfortunately, that made him think of her lips again.

He glared at the sand, which was pure white and finer than sugar. They were in a cove of a small bay, and the water was striped in aqua shades of turquoise, all the way out to a reef, where the water turned dark navy blue, and the waves broke, white-capped, over rocks.

"Well," he said, "I'll just head back."

"Do you ever just answer a question?"

"Sit, sit," Tandu said from behind them.

Drew swung around to look at him. While he had been looking out toward the sea, Tandu had emptied the wicker basket he carried. There was a blanket set up in the sand, and laid out on it was a bottle of wine, beaded with sweat, two wineglasses and two plates. There was a platter of blackened chicken, fresh fruit and golden, steaming croissants.

"What the hell?" Drew asked.

"Sit, sit—amens...amens."

"I'm not following," Drew said. He saw that

Becky had had no trouble whatsoever plopping herself down on the blanket. Had she forgotten she'd lost a whole day? She had to be seriously behind schedule.

"I make amens," Tandu said quietly, "for not doing first aid."

"Oh, *amends*," Drew said uncomfortably. "Really, it's not necessary at all. I have a ton of stuff to do. I'm not very hungry." This was a complete lie, though he had not realized quite how hungry he was until the food had *magically* appeared.

Tandu looked dejected that his offer was being refused.

"You very irritated with me," Tandu said sadly.

Becky caught his eye, lifted her shoulder— *come on, be a sport*—and patted the blanket. With a resigned shake of his head, Drew lowered himself onto the blanket. He bet if he ate one bite of this food that had been set out the spell would be complete.

"Look, I wasn't exactly irritated." This was as much a lie as the one about how he wasn't hungry, and he had a feeling Tandu was not easily fooled. "I was just a little surprised by a first aid man who doesn't like blood."

"Oh, yes," Tandu said happily. "Sit, sit, I fix."

"I am sitting. There's to nothing to fix." Except that Sainte Simone needed a new first aid attendant—before two hundred people descended on it would be good—but Drew found he did not have the heart to tell Tandu that.

Maybe the place was as magical as it looked, because he found himself unable to resist sitting beside Becky on the picnic blanket, though he told himself he had complied only because he did not want to disappoint Tandu, who had obviously misinterpreted his level of annoyance.

"I am not a first aid man," Tandu said. "Uh, how you say, medicine man? My family are healers. We see things."

"See things?" Drew asked. "I'm not following."

"Like a seer or a shaman?" Becky asked. She sounded thrilled.

Drew shot her a look. *Don't encourage him.* She ignored him. "Like what kind of things? Like the future?"

Drew groaned.

"Well, how did he know we needed a wedding site?" she challenged him.

"Because two hundred people are descending on this little piece of paradise for a marriage?"

She actually stuck one of her pointy little elbows in his ribs as if it was rude of him to point out the obvious.

"Yes, yes, like future," Tandu said, very pleased, missing or ignoring Drew's skepticism and not seeing Becky's dig in his ribs. "See things."

"So what do you see for the wedding?" Becky asked eagerly, leaning forward, as if she was going to put a great deal of stock in the answer.

Tandu looked off into the distance. He suddenly did not look like a smiling servant in a white shirt. Not at all. His expression was intense, and when he turned his gaze back to them, his liquid brown eyes did not seem soft or merry anymore.

"Unexpected things," he said softly. "Lots of surprises. Very happy, very happy wedding. Everybody happy. Babies. Many, many babies in the future."

Becky clapped her hands with delight. "Drew, you're going to be an uncle."

"How very terrifying," he said drily. "Since you can see things, Tandu, when is my brother arriving?"

"Not when you expect," Tandu said, without hesitation.

"Thanks. Tell me something I don't know."

Tandu appeared to take that as a challenge. He gazed off into the distance again. Finally he spoke.

"Broken hearts mended," Tandu said with satisfaction.

"Whose broken hearts?" Becky asked, her eyes wide. "The bride? The groom?"

"For Pete's sake," Drew snapped.

Tandu did not look at him, but gazed steadily and silently at Becky.

"Oh," Becky said, embarrassed. "I don't have a broken heart."

Tandu cocked his head, considering. Drew found himself listening with uncomfortable intentness.

"You left your brokenness in the water," Tandu told Becky. "What you thought was true never was."

She gasped softly, then turned faintly accusing eyes to Drew. "Did you tell him what I said about Jerry?"

He was amazed how much it stung that she thought he would break her confidence. That accusing look in her eyes should be a good thing—it might cool the sparks that had leaped up between them.

But he couldn't leave well enough alone. "Of course not," he said.

"Well, then how did he know?"

"He's a seer," Drew reminded her with a certain amount of satisfaction.

Tandu seemed to have not heard one word of this conversation.

"But you need to swim," he told Becky. "Not be afraid of water. Water here very, very good swimming. Safe. Best swimming beach right here."

"Oh, that's a good idea," she said, turning her head to look at the inviting water, "but I'm not prepared."

"Prepared?" Tandu said, surprised. "What to prepare?"

"I don't have a swimming suit," Becky told him.

"At all?" Drew asked, despite himself. "Who comes to the Caribbean without a swimming suit?"

"I'm not here to play," she said with a stern toss of her head.

"God forbid," he said, but he could not help but feel she was a woman who seemed to take life way too seriously. Which, of course, was not his problem.

"I don't actually own a swimming suit," she

said. "The nearest pool is a long way from
Moose Run. We aren't close to a lake."

"Ha. Born with swimming suit," Tandu told
her seriously. "Skin waterproof."

Drew watched with deep pleasure as the
crimson crept up her neck to her cheeks. "Ha-
ha," he said in an undertone, "that's what you
get for encouraging him."

"You swim," Tandu told her. "Eat first, then
swim. Mr. Drew help you."

"Naked swimming," Drew said. "Happy to
help when I can. Tandu, do you see skinny-
dipping in my future?"

There was that pointy little elbow in his ribs
again, quite a bit harder than it had been the
last time.

But before he could enjoy Becky's discomfort too much, suddenly Drew found himself
pinned in Tandu's intense gaze. "The heart that
is broken is yours, Mr. Drew?"

CHAPTER EIGHT

DREW JORDAN ORDERED himself to say no. No to magic. No to the light in Becky's eyes. And especially no to Tandu's highly invasive question. But instead of saying no, he found he couldn't speak at all, as if his throat was closing and his tongue was stuck to the roof of his mouth.

"They say a man is not given more than he can take, eh?" Tandu said.

If there was an expression on the face of the earth that Drew hated with his whole heart and soul it was that one, but he still found he could say nothing.

"But you were," Tandu said softly. "You were given more than you could take. You are a strong man. But not that strong, eh, Mr. Drew?"

His chest felt heavy. His throat felt as if it was closing. There was a weird stinging behind his eyes, as if he was allergic to the over-whelming scent of those flowers.

Without warning, he was back there.

He was seventeen years old. He was standing at the door of his house. It was the middle of the night. His feet and chest were bare and he had on pajama bottoms. He was blinking away sleep, trying to comprehend the stranger at the door of his house. The policeman said, "I'm sorry, son." And then Drew found out he wasn't anyone's son, not anymore.

Drew shook his head and looked at Tandu, fiercely.

"You heal now," Tandu said, not intimidated, as if it was an order. "You heal." And then suddenly Tandu was himself again, the easy-going grin on his face, his teeth impossibly perfect and white against the golden brown of his skin. His eyes were gentle and warm. "Eat, eat. Then swim. Then sunset."

And then he was gone.

"What was that about?" Becky asked him.

"I don't have a clue," he said. His voice sounded strange to him, choked and hoarse. "Creepy weirdness."

Becky was watching him as if she knew it was a lie. When had he become such a liar? He'd better give it up, he was terrible at it. He poured two glasses of wine, handed her one and tossed back the other. He set down the glass carefully.

"There. I've toasted the wedding spot. I'm going to go now." He didn't move.

"Have you?" she asked.

"Have I what? Toasted the wedding spot?"

"Had a heartbreak?" she asked softly, with concern.

And he felt, suddenly, as alone with his burdens as he had ever felt. He felt as if he could lay it all at her feet. He looked at the warmth and loveliness of her brushed-suede eyes. *You heal now.*

He reeled back from the invitation in her eyes. He was the most pragmatic of men. He was not under the enchantment of this beach, or Tandu's words, or her.

Not yet, an inner voice informed him cheerfully.

Not ever, he informed the inner voice with no cheer at all. He was not touching that food with its potential to weaken him even further. And no more wine.

"People like me," he said, forcing a cavalier ease into his voice.

She leaned toward him.

"We don't have hearts to break. I'm leaving now." Still, he did not move.

She looked as if she wanted to argue with that, but she took one look at his face and very wisely turned her attention to the chicken. "Is this burned?" she asked, poking one of the pieces gingerly with her fingertip.

"I think it's jerked, a very famous way of cooking on these islands." It felt like a relief to focus on the chicken instead of what was going on inside himself.

She took a piece and nibbled it. Her expression changed to one of complete awe. "You have to try it," she insisted. "You have to try it and tell me if it isn't the best thing you have ever tasted. Just one bite before you go."

Despite knowing this food probably had a spell woven right into it, he threw caution to the wind, picked up a leg of chicken and chomped into it. Just a few hours ago it definitely would have been the best thing he had ever tasted. But now that he was under a spell, he saw things differently.

Because the blackened jerk chicken quite possibly might have been the best thing he'd ever tasted, if he hadn't very foolishly sampled her lips when she had offered them yesterday afternoon.

"You might as well stay and eat," she said. She reached over and refilled his empty wineglass. "It would be a shame to let it go to waste."

He was not staying here, eating enchanted food in an enchanted cove with a woman who was clearly putting a spell on him. On the other hand, she was right. It would be a shame to let the food go to waste.

There was no such thing as spells, anyway. He picked up his second piece of chicken. He watched her delicately lick her fingertips.

"We don't have this kind of food in Moose Run," she said. "More's the pity."

"What kind of food do you have?" He was just being polite, he told himself, before he left her. He frowned. That second glass of wine could not be gone.

"We have two restaurants. We have the Main Street Diner which specializes in half-pound hamburgers and claims to have the best chocolate milk shake in all of Michigan."

"Claims?"

"I haven't tried all the chocolate milk shakes in Michigan," she said. "But believe me, I'm working on it."

He felt something relax within him. He should not be relaxing. He needed to keep his guard up. Still, he laughed at her earnest expression.

"And then we have Mr. Wang's All-You-Can-Eat Spectacular Smorgasbord."

"So, two restaurants. What else do you do for fun?"

She looked uncomfortable. It was none of his business, he told himself firmly. Why did he care if it was just as he'd suspected? She did not have nearly enough fun going on in her life. Not that it was any concern of his.

"Is there a movie theater?" he coaxed her.

"Yes. And don't forget the church picnic."

"And dancing on the grass," he supplied.

"I'm not much for the church socials, actually. I don't really like dancing."

"So what do you like?"

She hesitated, and then met his eyes. "I'm sure you are going to think I am the world's most boring person, but you know what I really do for fun?"

He felt as if he was holding his breath for some reason. Crazy to hope the answer was going to involve kissing. Not that anyone would consider that boring, would they? Was his wineglass full again? He took a sip.

"I read," she said, in a hushed whisper, as if

she was in a confessional. She sighed. "I love to read."

What a relief! Reading, not kissing! It should have seemed faintly pathetic, but somehow, just like the rest of her, it seemed real. In an amusement park world where everyone was demanding to be entertained constantly, by bigger things and better amusements and wilder rides and greater spectacles, by things that stretched the bounds of what humans were intended to do, it seemed lovely that Becky had her own way of being in the world, and that something so simple as opening a book could make someone contented.

She was bracing herself, as if she expected him to be scornful. It made him wonder if the ex-beau had been one of those put-down kind of guys.

"I can actually picture you out in a hammock on a sunny afternoon," he said. "It sounds surprisingly nice."

"At this time of year, it's a favorite chair. On my front porch. We still have front porches in Moose Run."

He could picture a deeply shaded porch, and a sleepy street, and hear the sound of birds. This, too, struck him as deliciously simple in a complicated world. "What's your favorite book?" he asked.

"I have to pick one?" she asked with mock horror.

"Let me put it differently. If you had to recommend a book to someone who hardly ever reads, which one would it be?"

And somehow it was that easy. The food was disappearing and so was the wine, and she was telling him about her favorite books and authors, and he was telling her about surfing the big waves and riding his motorbike on the Pacific Coast Highway between LA and San Francisco.

The fight seemed to ease out of him, and the wariness. The urgent need to be somewhere else seemed silly. Drew felt himself relaxing. Why not enjoy it? It was no big deal. Tomorrow his crew would be here. He would immerse himself in his work. He could enjoy this last evening with Becky before that happened, couldn't he?

Who would have ever guessed it would be so easy to be with a man like this? Becky thought. The conversation was comfortable between them. There was so much work that needed to be done on Allie's wedding, and she had already lost a precious day. Still, she had never felt less inclined to do work.

But as comfortable as it all was, she could feel a little nudge of disappointment. How could they go from that electrifying kiss, to this?

Not that she wanted the danger of that kiss again, but she certainly didn't want him to think she was a dull small-town girl whose idea of an exciting evening was sitting out on her front porch reading until the fireflies came out.

Dinner was done. The wine bottle was lying on its side, empty. All that was left of the chicken was bones, and all that was left of the croissants were a few golden crumbs. As she watched, Drew picked one of those up on his fingertip and popped it in his mouth.

How could such a small thing be so darned sexy?

In her long pants and long-sleeved shirt, Becky was suddenly aware of feeling way too warm. And overdressed. She was aware of being caught in the enchantment of Sainte Simone and this beautiful beach. She longed to be free of encumbrances.

Like clothing? she asked herself, appalled,

but not appalled enough to stop the next words that came out of her mouth.

"Let's go for that swim after all," she said. She tried to sound casual, but her heart felt as if she had just finished running a marathon.

"I really need to go." He said it without any kind of conviction. "Are you going to swim in nature's bathing suit?"

"Don't be a pervert!"

"I'm not. Tandu suggested it. One-hundred-percent waterproof."

"Don't look," she said.

"Sure. I'll stop breathing while I'm at it."

What was she doing? she asked herself.

For once in her life, she was acting on a whim, that's what she was doing. For once in her life she was being bold, that's what she was doing. For once in her life, she was throwing convention to the wind, she was doing what she wanted to do. She was not leaving him with the impression she was a dull small-town girl who had spent her whole life with her nose buried in a book. Even if she had been!

She didn't want that to be the whole truth about her anymore, and not just because of him, either. Because the incident in the water yesterday, that moment when she had looked her own death in the face and somehow been spared, had left her with a longing for second chances.

She stood up and turned her back to him. Becky took a deep breath and peeled her shirt over her head, then unbuckled her slacks and stepped out of them. She had on her luxurious Rembrandt's Drawing brand underwear. The underwear was a matching set, a deep shade of turquoise not that different from the water. It was as fashionable as most bathing suits, and certainly more expensive.

She glanced over her shoulder, and his expression—stunned, appreciative, approving—made her run for the water. She splashed in up to her knees, and then threw herself in. The water closed over her head, and unlike yesterday afternoon, it felt wonderful in the heat of the early evening, cool and silky as a caress on her nearly naked skin.

She surfaced, then paddled out and found her footing when she was up to her neck in water, her underwear hidden from him. She turned to look at where he was still sitting on the blanket. Even from here, she could see the heat in his eyes.

Oh, girlfriend, she thought, *you do not know what you are playing with.* But the thing about letting a bolder side out was that it was very hard to stuff it back in, like trying to get a jack-in-the-box back in its container.

"Come in," she called. "It's glorious."

He stood up slowly and peeled his shirt off. She held her breath. It was her turn to be stunned, appreciative and approving.

She had seen him without his shirt already when he had sacrificed it to doctor her leg. But this was different. She wasn't in shock, or in pain, or bleeding all over the place.

Becky was aware, as she had been when she had first laid eyes on him, that he was the most beautifully made of men. Broad shouldered and deep chested, muscular without being muscle-bound. He could be an actor or a model, because he had that mysterious something that made her—and probably every other woman on earth—feel as if she could look at him endlessly, drink in his masculine perfection as if he was a long, cool drink of water and she was dying of thirst.

Was he going to take off his shorts? She was aware she was holding her breath. But no, he kicked off his shoes and, with the khaki shorts safely in place, ran toward the water. Like she had done, he ran in up to about his thighs and then she watched as he dived beneath the surface.

"I didn't peg you for shy," she told him when he surfaced close to her.

He lifted an eyebrow at her.

"I've seen men's underwear before. I'm from Moose Run, not the convent."

"You've mentioned you weren't a nun once before," he said. "What's with the fascination with nuns?"

"You just seem to think because I'm small town I'm prim and proper. You didn't have to get your shorts all wet to save my sensibilities."

"I don't wear underwear."

Her mouth fell open. She could feel herself turning crimson. He laughed, delighted at her discomfort.

"How are your sensibilities doing now?" he asked her.

"Fine," she squeaked. But they both knew it was a lie, and he laughed.

"Come on," he said, shaking the droplets of water from his hair. "I'll race you to those rocks."

"That's ridiculous. I don't have a hope of winning."

"I know," he said fiendishly.

"I get a head start."

"All right."

"A big one."

"Okay, you tell me when I can go."

She paddled her way toward the rocks. When it seemed there was no chance he could catch her, she called, "Okay, go."

She could hear him coming up behind her. She paddled harder. He grabbed her foot!

"Hey!" She went under the water. He let go of her foot, and when she surfaced, he had surged by her and was touching the rock.

"You cheater," she said indignantly.

"You're the cheater. What kind of head start was that?"

"Watch who you are calling a cheater." She reached back her arm and splashed him, hard. He splashed her back. The war was on.

Tandu had been so right. She needed to leave whatever fear she had remaining in the water.

And looking at Drew's face, she realized, her fear was not about drowning. It was about caring for someone else, as if pain was an inherent ingredient to that.

Becky could see that if she had not let go enough in life, neither had he. Seeing him like this, playful, his face alight with laugher and mischief, she realized he did carry some burden, like a weight, just as Tandu had suggested. Drew had put down his burden for a bit, out here in the water, and she was glad she had encouraged him to come swim with her.

She wondered what his terrible burden was. Could he really have been given more than he thought he could handle? He seemed so unbelievably strong. But then again, wasn't that what made strength, being challenged to your outer limits? She wondered if he would ever confide in her, but then he splashed her in the face and took off away from her, and she took chase, and the serious thoughts were gone.

A half hour later, exhausted, they dragged themselves up on the beach. Just as he had promised, the trades came up, and it was surprisingly chilly on her wet skin and underwear. She tried to pull her clothes over her wet underwear, but it was more difficult than she thought. Finally, with her clothes clinging to her uncomfortably, she turned to him.

He had pulled his shirt back on over his wet chest and was putting the picnic things back in the basket.

"We have to go," she said. "I feel guilty."

"Tut-tut," he said. "There's that nun thing again. But I have to go, too. My crew is arriving first thing in the morning. I'd like to have things set up so we can get right to work. You're a terrible influence on me, Sister English."

"Sister Simone, to you."

He didn't appear to be leaving, and neither did she.

"I am so far behind in what I need to get done," Becky said. "I didn't expect to be here this long. If I go to work right now, I can still make a few phone calls. What time do you think it is in New York?"

"Look what I just found."

Did he ever just answer the question?

He had been rummaging in the picnic basket and he held up two small mason jars that looked as if they were filled with whipped cream and strawberries.

"What is that?" Knowing the time in New York suddenly didn't seem important at all.

"I think it's dessert."

She licked her lips. He stared at them, before looking away.

"I guess a little dessert wouldn't hurt," she said. Her voice sounded funny, low and seductive, as if she had said something faintly naughty.

"Just sit in the sand," he suggested. "We'll wrap the picnic blanket over our shoulders. We might as well eat dessert and watch the sun go down. What's another half hour now?"

They were going to sit shoulder to shoulder

under a blanket eating dessert and watching the sun go down? It was better than any book she had ever read! The time in New York— and all her other responsibilities—did a slow fade-out, as if it was the end of a movie.

CHAPTER NINE

BECKY PLUNKED HERSELF down like a dog at obedience class who was eager for a treat. Drew picked up the blanket and placed it carefully over her shoulders, then sat down in the sand beside her and pulled part of the blanket over his own shoulders. His shoulder felt warm and strong where her skin was touching it. The chill left her almost instantly.

He pried the lid off one of the jars and handed it to her with a spoon.

"Have you ever been to Hawaii?" He took the lid off the other jar.

"No, I'm sorry to say I haven't been. Have you?"

"I've done jobs there. It's very much like this, the climate, the foliage, the breathtaking beauty. Everything stops at sunset. Even if you're still working against an impossible deadline, you just stop and face the sun. It's like every single person stops and every single thing stops. This stillness comes over everything. It's like the deepest form of gratitude I've ever experienced. It's this thank-you to life."

"I feel that right now," she said, with soft reverence. "Maybe because I nearly drowned, I feel so intensely alive and so intensely grateful."

No need to mention sharing this evening with him might have something to do with feeling so intensely alive.

"Me, too," he said softly.

Was it because of her he felt this way? She could feel the heat of his shoulder where it was touching hers. She desperately wanted to kiss him again. She gobbled up strawberries and cream instead. It just made her long, even more intensely, for the sweetness of his lips.

"I am going to hell in a handbasket," she muttered, but still she snuggled under the blanket and looked at where the sun, now a huge orb of gold, was hovering over the ocean.

He shot her a look. "Why would you say that?"

Because she was enjoying him so much, when she, of all people, was so well versed in all the dangers of romance.

"Because I am sitting here watching the sun go down when I should be getting to work," she clarified with a half-truth. "I knew Allie's faith in me was misplaced."

"Why would you say that?"

"I'm just an unlikely choice for such a huge undertaking."

"So, why did she pick you, then?"

"I hadn't seen her, or even had a note from her, since she moved away from Moose Run." Becky sighed and pulled the blanket tighter around her shoulders. "Everyone in Moose Run claims to have been friends with Allison Anderson *before* she became Allie Ambrosia the movie star, but really they weren't. Allison was lonely and different, and many of those people who now claim to have been friends with her were actually exceptionally intolerant of her eccentricities.

"Her mom must have been one of the first internet daters. She came to Moose Run and moved in with Pierce Clemens, which anybody could have told her was a bad bet. Allie, with her body piercings and colorful hair and hippie skirts, was just way too exotic for Moose Run. She only lived there for two years, and she and I only had a nodding acquaintance for most of that time. We were in the same grade, but I was in advanced classes."

"That's a surprise," he teased drily.

"You could have knocked me over with a feather when I got an out-of-the-blue phone call from her a couple of weeks ago and she outlined her ambitious plans. She told me she was putting together a guest list of two hundred people and that she wanted it to be so much more than a wedding. She wants her guests to have an *experience.* The island was hers for an entire week after the wedding, and she wanted all the guests to stay and have fun, either relaxing or joining in on organized activities.

"You know what she suggested for activities? Volleyball tournaments and wienie roasts around a campfire at night, maybe fireworks! You're from there. Does that strike you as Hollywood?"

"No," he said. "Not at all. Hollywood would be Jet Skis during the day and designer dresses at night. It would be entertainment by Cirque and Shania and wine tasting and spa treatments on the beach."

"That's what I thought. But she was adamant about what she wanted. I couldn't help but think that Allie's ideas of fun, despite this exotic island setting, are those of a girl who had been largely excluded from the teen cliques who went together to the Fourth of July activities. She seems, talking to her, to be more in sync with the small-town tastes of Moose Run than with lifestyles of the rich and famous."

"It actually makes me like her more," he said reluctantly.

"I asked her if what she wanted was like summer camp for adults, to make sure I was getting it right. She said—" Becky imitated the famous actress's voice "—'Exactly! I knew I could count on you to get it right.'"

Drew chuckled at Becky's imitation of Allie, which encouraged her to be even more foolish. She did both voices, as if she was reading for several parts in a play.

"Allie, I'm not sure I'm up to this. My event company has become the go-to company for local weddings and anniversaries, but— 'Of course you are up to it, do you think I don't do my homework? You did that great party for the lawyer's kid. Ponies!'

"She said *ponies* with the same enthusiasm she said *fireworks* with," Becky told Drew ruefully. "I think she actually wanted ponies. So I said, 'Um…it would be hard to get ponies to an island—and how did you know that? About the party for Mr. Williams's son?' And she said, 'I do my research. I'm not quite as flaky as the roles I get might make you think.' Of course, I told her I never thought she was flaky, but she cut me off and told me she was sending a deposit. I tried to talk her out of it. I said a six-week timeline was way too short to throw together a wedding for two hundred people. I told her I would have to delegate all my current contracts to take it on. She just insisted. She said she would make it worth my while. I told her I just wasn't sure, and she said she was, and that I was perfect for the job."

"You were trying to get out of the opportunity of a lifetime?" Drew weighed in, amused.

"Was I ever. But then her lighthearted delivery kind of changed and she said I was the only reason she survived Moose Run at all. She asked me if I remembered the day we became friends."

"Did you?"

"Pretty hard to forget. A nasty group of boys had her backed into the corner in that horrid place at the high school where we used to all go to smoke.

"I mean, I didn't go there to smoke. I was Moose Run High's official Goody Two-shoes."

"No kidding," he said drily. "Do not elbow my ribs again. They are seriously bruised."

They sat there in companionable silence for a few minutes. The sun demanded their stillness and their silence. The sunset was at its most glorious now, painting the sky around it in shades of orange and pink that were reflecting on a band on the ocean, that seemed to lead a pathway of light right to them. Then the sun was gone, leaving only an amazing pastel palette staining the sky.

"Go on," he said.

Becky thought she was talking too much. Had they really drunk that whole bottle of wine between the two of them? Still, it felt nice to have someone to talk to, someone to listen.

"I was taking a shortcut to the library—"

"Naturally," he said with dry amusement.

"And I came across Bram Butler and his gang tormenting poor Allie. I told them to cut it out.

"Allie remembers me really giving it to them. She told me that for a long time she has always thought of me as having the spirit of a gladiator."

"I'll attest to that," he said. "I have the bruises on my ribs to prove it." And then his tone grew more serious. "And you never gave up in the water yesterday, either."

"That was because of you. Believe me, I am the little bookworm I told you I was earlier. I do not have the spirit of a gladiator."

Though she did have some kind of unexpected spirit of boldness that had made her, very uncharacteristically, rip off her clothes and go into the water.

"How many guys were there?"

"Hmm, it was years ago, but I think maybe four. No, five."

"What were they doing?"

"They kind of had her backed up against a wall. She was quite frightened. I think that stupid Bram was trying to kiss her. He's always been a jerk. He's my second cousin."

"And you just waded right in there, with five high school guys being jerks? That seems brave."

She could not allow herself to bask in his admiration, particularly since it was undeserved.

"I didn't exactly wade right in there. I used the Moose Run magic words."

"Which were?"

"Bram Butler, you stop it right now or I'll tell your mother."

He burst out laughing, and then so did she.

She noticed that it had gotten quite dark. The wind had died. Already stars were rising in the sky.

"Allie and I hung out a bit after that," she said. "She was really interesting. At that time, she wanted to be a clothing designer. We used to hole up in my room and draw dresses."

"What kind of dresses?"

"Oh, you know. Prom. Evening. That kind of thing. Allie and her mom moved away shortly after that. She said we would keep in touch— that she would send me her new address and phone number—but she never did."

"You and Allie drew wedding dresses, didn't you?"

"What would make you say that?" Becky could feel a blush rising, but why should she have to apologize for her younger self?

"I'm trying to figure out if she has some kind of wedding fantasy that my brother just happened into."

"Lots of young women have romantic fantasies. And then someone comes along to disillusion them."

"Like your Jerry," he said. "Tell me about that."

"So little to tell," she said wryly. "We lived down the street from one another, we started the first grade together. When we were seventeen he asked me to go to the Fourth of July celebrations with him. He held my hand. We kissed. And there you have it, my whole future mapped out for me. We were just together after that. I wanted exactly what I grew up with, until my dad left. Up until then my family had been one of those solid, dull families that makes the world feel so, so safe.

"An illusion," she said sadly. "It all ended up being such an illusion, but I felt determined to prove it could be real. Jerry went away to college and I started my own business, and it just unraveled, bit by bit. It's quite humiliating to have a major breakup in a small town."

"I bet."

"When I think about it, the humiliation actually might have been a lot harder to handle than the fact that I was not going to share my life with Jerry. It was like a second blow. I had just barely gotten over being on the receiving end of the pitying looks over my dad's scandal."

"Are you okay with your dad's relationship now?"

"I wish I was. But they still live in Moose Run, and I have an adorable little sister who I am pathetically jealous of. They seem so happy. My mom is still a mess. Aside from working in the hardware store, she'd never even had a job."

"And you rushed in to become the family breadwinner," he said.

"It's not a bad thing, is it?"

"An admirable thing. And kind of sad."

His hand found hers and he gave it a squeeze. He didn't let go again.

"Were you thinking of Jerry when you were drawing those dresses?" he finally asked softly.

"No," she said slowly, "I don't think I was."

She suddenly remembered one dress in particular that Allie had drawn. *This is your wedding dress*, she had proclaimed, giving it to Becky.

It had been a confection, sweetheart neckline, fitted bodice, layers and layers and layers of filmy fabric flowing out in that full skirt with an impossible train. The dress had been the epitome of her every romantic notion. Becky had been able to picture herself in that dress, swirling in front of a mirror, giggling. But she had never, not even once, pictured herself in that dress walking down an aisle toward Jerry.

When Jerry had broken it to her that her "business was changing her"—in other words, he could not handle her success—and he wanted his ring back, she had never taken that drawing from where it was tucked in the back of one of her dresser drawers.

"I've talked too much," she said. "It must have been the wine."

"I don't think you talked too much."

"I usually don't confide in people so readily." She suddenly felt embarrassed. "Your name should be a clue."

"To?"

"You *drew* my secrets right out of me."

"Ah."

"We have to go now," she said.

"Yes, we do," he said.

"Before something happens," she said softly.

"Especially before that," he agreed just as softly.

Her hand was still in his. Their shoulders were touching. The breeze was lifting the leathery fronds of the palm trees and they were whispering songs without words. The sky was now almost completely black, and finding their way back was not going to be easy.

"Really," Becky said. "We need to go."

"Really," he agreed. "We do.

Neither of them moved.

CHAPTER TEN

DREW ORDERED HIMSELF to get up and leave this beach. But it was one of those completely irresistible moments: the stars winking on in the sky, their shoulders touching, the taste of strawberries and cream on his lips, the gentle lap of the waves against the shore, her small hand resting within the sanctuary of his larger one.

He turned slightly to look at her. She was turning to look at him.

It seemed like the most natural thing in the world to drop his head over hers, to taste her lips again.

Her arms came up and twined around his neck. Her lips were soft and pliant and welcoming.

He could taste everything she was in that kiss. She was bookish. And she was bold. She was simple, and she was complex. She was, above all else, a forever kind of girl.

It was that knowledge that made him untangle her hands from around his neck, to force his lips away from the soft promise of hers.

You heal now.

He swore under his breath, scrambled to his feet. "I'm sorry," he said.

"Are you?"

Well, not really. "Look, Becky, we have known each other for a shockingly short period of time. Obviously circumstances have made us feel things about each other a little too quickly."

She looked unconvinced.

"I mean, in Moose Run, you probably have a date or two before you kiss like that."

"What about in LA?"

He thought about how fast things could go in Los Angeles and how superficial that was, and how he was probably never going to be satisfied with it again. Less than forty-eight hours, and Becky English, bookworm, was changing everything in his world.

What was his world going to look like in two weeks if this kept up?

The answer was obvious. This could not keep up.

"Look, Becky, I obviously like you. And find you extremely attractive."

Did she look pleased? He did not want her to look pleased!

"There is obviously some kind of chemistry going on between us."

She looked even more pleased.

"But both of us have jobs to do. We have very little time to do those jobs in. We can't afford a, um, complication like this."

She stared at him, uncomprehending.

"It's not professional, Becky," he said gruffly. "Kissing on the job is not professional."

She looked as if he had slapped her. And then she just looked crushed.

"Oh," she stammered. "Of course, you're right."

He felt a terrible kind of self-loathing that she was taking it on, as if it were her fault.

She pulled herself together and jumped up, doing what he suspected she always did. Trying to fix the whole world. Her clothes were still wet. Her pink blouse looked as though red roses were blooming on it where it was clinging to that delectable set of underwear that he should never have seen, and was probably never going to be able to get out of his mind.

"I don't know what's gotten into me. It must still be the aftereffects of this afternoon. And the wine. I want you to know I don't usually rip my clothes off around men. In fact, that's extremely uncharacteristic. And I'm usually not such a blabbermouth. Not at all."

Her voice was wobbling terribly.

"No, it's not you," he rushed to tell her. "It's not. It's me, I—"

"I've given you the impression I'm—what did you call it earlier—wanton!"

"I told you at the time I was overstating it. I told you that was the wrong word."

She held up her hand, stopping him. "No, I take responsibility. You don't know how sorry I am."

And then she rushed by him, found the path through the darkened jungle and disappeared.

Perfect, he thought. He'd gotten rid of her before things got dangerously out of control. But it didn't feel perfect. He felt like a bigger jerk than the chicken they had eaten for supper.

She had fled up that path—away from him—with extreme haste, probably hoping to keep the truth from him. That she was crying.

But that's what I am, Drew told himself. He was a jerk. Just ask his brother, who not only wasn't arriving on the island, but who also was not taking his phone calls.

The truth was, Drew Jordan sucked at relationships. It was good Becky had run off like that, for her own protection, and his. It would have been better if he could have thought of a way to make her believe it was his fault instead of hers, though.

Sitting there, alone, in the sand, nearly choking on his own self-loathing, Drew thought of his mother. He could picture her: the smile, the way she had made him feel, that way she had of cocking her head and listening so intently when he was telling her something. He realized the scent he had detected earlier had reminded him of her perfume.

The truth was, he was shocked to be thinking of her. Since that day he had become both parents to his younger brother, he had tried not to think of his mom and dad. It was just too painful. Losing them—everything, really, his whole world—was what life had given him that was too much to bear.

But the tears in Becky's eyes that she had been holding back so valiantly, and the scent in the air, made him think of his mother. Only in his mind, his mother wasn't cocking her head, listening intently to him with that soft look of wonder that only a mother can have for her offspring.

No, it felt as if his mother was somehow near

him, but that her hands were on her hips and she was looking at him with total exasperation.

His mother, he knew, would never have approved of the fact he had made that decent, wholesome young woman from Moose Run, Michigan, cry. She would be really angry with him if he excused his behavior by saying, *But it was for her own good.* His mother, if she was here, would remind him of all the hurt that Becky had already suffered at the hands of men.

She would show him Becky, trying to keep her head up as her father pushed a stroller down the main street of Moose Run, as news got out that the wedding planner's own wedding was a bust.

Sitting there in the sand with the stars coming out over him, Drew felt he was facing some hard truths about himself. Would his mother even approve of the man he had become? Work-obsessed, so emotionally unavailable he had driven his brother right out of his life and into the first pair of soft arms that offered comfort. His mother wouldn't like it one bit that not only was he failing to protect his brother from certain disaster, his brother would not even talk to him.

"So," he asked out loud, "what would you have me do?"

Be a better man.

It wasn't her voice. It was just the gentle breeze stirring the palm fronds. It was just the waves lapping onshore. It was just the call of the night birds.

But is that what her voice had become? Everything? Was his mother's grace and goodness now in everything? Including him?

Drew scrambled out of the sand. He picked up the picnic basket and the blanket and began to run.

"Becky! Becky!"

When he caught up with her, he was breathless. She was walking fast, her head down.

"Becky," he said, and then softly, "Please."

She spun around. She stuck her chin up in the air. But she could not hide the fact that he was right. She had been crying.

"I didn't mean to hurt your feelings," he said. "I'm the one in the wrong here, not you."

"Thank you," she said icily. "That is very chivalrous of you. However the facts speak for themselves."

Chivalrous. Who used that in a sentence? And why did it make him feel as if he wanted to set down the picnic basket, gather her in his arms and hold her hard?

"Facts?"

"Yes, facts," she said in that clipped tone of voice. "They speak for themselves."

"They do?"

She nodded earnestly. "It seems to me I've just dragged you along with my *wanton* behavior, kissing you, tearing off my clothes. You were correct. It is not professional. And it won't be happening again."

He knew that it not happening again was a good thing, so why did he feel such a sense of loss?

"Becky, I handled that badly."

"There's a good way to handle 'keep your lips off me'?"

He had made her feel rejected. He had done to her what every other man in her life had done to her: given her the message that somehow she didn't measure up, she wasn't good enough.

He rushed to try to repair the damage.

"It's not that I don't want your lips on me," he said. "I do. I mean I don't. I mean we can't. I mean I won't."

She cocked her head, and looked askance at him.

"Do I sound like an idiot?" he said.

"Yes," she said, unforgivingly.

"What I'm trying to say, Becky, is I'm not used to women like you."

"What kind of women are you used to?"

"Guess," he said in a low voice.

She did not appear to want to guess.

He raked his hand through his hair, trying desperately to think of a way to make her get it that would somehow erase those tearstains from her cheeks.

"I'm scared I'll hurt you," he said, his voice gravelly in his own ears. "I don't think it's a good idea to move this fast. Let's back up a step or two. Let's just be friends. First."

He had no idea where that *first* had come from. It implied there would be something following the friendship. But really, that was impossible. And he just had to get through what remained of two weeks without hurting her any more than he already had. He could play at being the better man for eleven damn days. He was almost sure of it.

"Do you ever answer a question?" she asked. "What kind of women are you used to?"

"Ones who are as shallow as me," he said.

"You aren't shallow!"

"You don't know that about me."

"I do," she said firmly.

He sucked in his breath and tried again. Why was she insisting on seeing him as a better man when he did not deserve that? "Ones who don't expect happily-ever-after."

"Oh."

"You see, Becky, my parents died when I was seventeen." *Shut up*, he ordered himself. *Stop it.* "It broke something in me. The sense of loss was just as Tandu said this afternoon. It was too great to bear. When I've had relationships, and it's true, I have, they have been deliberately superficial."

Becky went very still. Her eyes looked wide and beautiful in the starlight that filtered through the thick leaves of the jungle. She took a step toward him. And she reached up and laid the palm of her hand on his cheek.

Her touch was extraordinary. He had to shut his eyes against his reaction to the tenderness in it. In some ways it was more intimate than the kisses they had shared.

"Because you cannot handle one more loss," she guessed softly.

Drew opened his eyes and stared at Becky. It felt as if she could see his soul and was not the least frightened by what she saw there.

This was going sideways! He was not going

to answer that. He could not. If he answered that, he would want to lay his head on her shoulder and feel her hand in his hair. He would want to suck up her tenderness like a dry sponge sucking up moisture. If he answered that he would become weak, instead of what he needed to be most.

He needed to be strong. Since he'd been seventeen years old, he had needed to be strong. And it wasn't until just this minute he was seeing that as a burden he wanted to lay down.

"I agree," she said softly, dropping her hand away from his cheek. "We just need to be friends."

His relief was abject. She got it. He was too damaged to be any good for a girl like her.

Only then she went and spoiled his relief by standing on her tiptoes and kissing him on the cheek where her hand had lay with such tender healing. She whispered something in his ear.

And he was pretty sure it was the word *first*.

And then she turned and scampered across the moonlit lawn to the castle door and disappeared inside it.

And he had to struggle not to touch his cheek, where the tenderness of her kiss lingered like a promise.

You heal now.

But he couldn't. He knew that. He could do his best to honor the man his mother had raised him to be, to not cause Becky any more harm, but he knew that his own salvation was beyond what he could hope for.

Because really in the end, for a man like him, wasn't hope the most dangerous thing of all?

CHAPTER ELEVEN

BECKY LISTENED TO the sound of hammers, the steady *ratta-tat-tat* riding the breeze through the open window of her office. When had that sound become like music to her?

She told herself, sternly, she could not give in to the temptation, but it was useless. It was as if a cord circled her waist and tugged her toward the window.

This morning, Drew's crew had arrived, but not his brother. They had arrived ready to work, and in hours the wedding pavilion was taking shape on the emerald green expanse of the front lawn. They'd dug holes and poured the cement they had mixed by hand out of bags. Then they had set the posts—which had arrived by helicopter—into those holes.

She had heard helicopters delivering supplies all morning. It sounded like a MASH unit around here.

Now she peeped out the window. In all that activity, her eyes sought him. Her heart went to her throat. Drew, facing the ocean, was straddling a beam. He had to be fifteen feet off the ground, his legs hanging into nothingness. He had a baseball cap on backward and his shirt off.

His skin was sun-kissed and perfect, his back broad and powerful. He was a picture of male strength and confidence.

She could barely breathe he was so amazing to look at. It was also wonderful to be able to look at him without his being aware of it! She could study the sleek lines of his naked back at her leisure.

"You have work to do," she told herself. Drew, as if he sensed someone watching, turned and glanced over his shoulder, directly at her window. She drew back into the shadows, embarrassed, and pleased, too. Was he looking to glimpse her? Did it fill him with this same sense of delight? Anticipation? Longing?

Reluctantly, she turned her back to the scene, but only long enough to try to drag her desk over to the window. She could multitask. The desk was very heavy. She grunted with exertion.

"Miss Becky?" Tandu was standing in the doorway with a tray. "Why you miss lunch?"

"Oh, I—" For some reason she had felt shy about lunch, knowing that Drew and his crew would be eating in the dining room. Despite their agreement last night to be friends, her heart raced out of control when she thought of his rescue of her, and eating dinner with him on the picnic blanket last night, and swimming with him. But mostly, she thought of how their lips had met. Twice.

How was she going to choke down a sandwich around him? How was she going to behave appropriately with his crew looking on? Anybody with a heartbeat would take one look at her—them—and know that something primal was sizzling in the air between them.

This was what she had missed by being with Jerry for so long. She had missed all the years when she should have been learning the delicate nuances of how to conduct a relationship with a member of the opposite sex.

Not that it was going to be a relationship. A friendship. She thought of Drew's lips. She wondered how a friendship was going to be possible.

There must be a happy medium between

wanton and so shy she couldn't even eat lunch with him!

"What you doing?" Tandu asked, looking at the desk she had managed to move about three feet across the room.

"The breeze!" she said, too emphatically. "I thought I might get a better breeze if I moved the desk."

Tandu set down the lunch tray. With his help it was easier to wrestle the big piece of furniture into its new location.

He looked out the window. "Nice view," he said with wicked amusement. "Eat lunch, enjoy the view. Then you are needed at helicopter pad. Cargo arriving. Many, many boxes."

"I have a checklist. I'll be down shortly. And Tandu, could you think of a few places for wedding photographs? I mean, the beaches are lovely, but if I could preview a few places for the photographer, that would be wonderful."

"Know exactly the place," he said delightedly. "Waterfall."

"Yes!" she said.

"I'll draw you a map."

"Thank you. A waterfall!"

"Now eat. Enjoy the view."

She did eat, and she did enjoy the view. It was actually much easier to get to work when she could just glance up and watch Drew, rather than making a special trip away from her desk and to the window.

Later that afternoon, she headed down to the helicopter loading dock with her checklist and began sorting through the boxes and muttering to herself.

"Candles? Check. Centerpieces? Check."

"Hi there." She swung around.

Drew was watching her, a little smile playing across his handsome features.

"Hello." Oh, God, did she have to sound so formal and geeky?

"Do you always catch your tongue between your teeth like that when you are lost in thought?"

She hadn't been aware she was doing it, and pulled her tongue back into her mouth. He laughed. She blushed.

"The pavilion is looking great," she said, trying to think of something—anything—to say. She was as tongue-tied as if she were a teenager meeting her secret crush unexpectedly at the supermarket!

"Yeah, my guys are pretty amazing, aren't they?"

She had not really spared a glance to any of the other guys. "Amazing," she agreed.

"I just thought I'd check and see if the fabric for draping the pavilion has arrived. I need to come up with a method for hanging it."

"I'll look."

But he was already sorting through boxes, tossing them with easy strength. "This might be it. It's from a fabric store. There's quite a few boxes here." He took a box cutter out of his shirt pocket and slit open one of the boxes. "Come see."

She sidled over to him. She could feel the heat radiating off him as they stood side by side.

"Yes, that's it."

He hefted up one of the boxes onto his shoulder. "I'll send one of the guys over for the rest."

She stood there. That was going to be the whole encounter. *Very professional*, she congratulated herself.

"You want to come weigh in on how to put it up?" he called over his shoulder.

And she threw professionalism to the wind and scampered after him like a puppy who had been given a second chance at affection.

"Hey, guys," he called. "Team meeting. Fabric's here."

His guys, four of them, gathered around.

"Becky, Jared, Jason, Josh and Jimmy."

"The J series," one of them announced. "Brothers. I'm the good-looking one, Josh." He gave a little bow.

"But I'm the strong one," Jimmy announced.

"And I'm the smart one."

"I'm the romantic," Jared said, and stepped forward, picked up her hand and kissed it, to groans from his brothers. "You are a beauty, me lady. Do you happen to be available? I see no rings, so—"

"That's enough," Drew said.

His tone had no snap to it, at all, only firmness, but Becky did not miss how quickly Jared stepped back from her, or the surprised looks exchanged between the brothers.

She liked seeing Drew in this environment. It was obvious his crew of brothers didn't just respect him, they adored him. She soon saw why.

"Let's see what we have here," Drew said. He opened a box and yards and yards of filmy white material spilled out onto the ground.

He was a natural leader, listening to all the brothers' suggestions about how to attach and drape the fabric to the pavilion poles they had worked all morning installing.

"How about you, Becky?" Drew asked her. She was flattered that her opinion mattered, too. "I think you should put some kind of bar on those side beams. Long bars, like towel bars, and then thread the fabric through them."

"We have a winner," one of the guys shouted, and they all clapped and went back to work.

"I'll hang the first piece and you can see if it works," Drew said.

With amazing ingenuity he had fabricated a bar in no time. And then he shinnied up a ladder that was leaning on a post and attached the first bar to the beam. And then he did the same on the other side.

"The moment of truth," he called from up on the wall.

She opened the box and he leaned way down to take the fabric from her outstretched hand. Once he had it, he threaded it through the first bar, then came down from the ladder, trailing a line of wide fabric behind him. He went up the ladder on the other side of what would soon look like a pavilion, and threaded the fabric through there. The panel was about three feet wide and dozens of feet long. He came down to the ground and passed her the fabric end.

"You do it," he said.

She tugged on it until the fabric lifted toward the sky, and then began to tighten. Finally, the first panel was in place. The light, filmy, pure-white fabric formed a dreamy roof above them, floating walls on either side of them. Only it was better than walls and a roof because of the way the light was diffused through it, and the way it moved like a living thing in the most gentle of breezes.

"Just like a canopy bed," he told her with satisfaction.

"You know way too much about that," she teased him.

"Actually," he said, frowning at the fabric, "come to think of it, it doesn't really look like a canopy bed. It looks like—"

He snatched up the hem of fabric and draped it over his shoulder. "It looks like a toga."

She burst out laughing.

He struck a pose. "'To be or not to be…'" he said.

"I don't want to be a geek…" she began.

"Oh, go ahead—be a geek. It comes naturally to you."

That stung, but even with it stinging, she couldn't let *To be or not to be* go unchallenged. "'To be or not to be' is Shakespeare," she told him. "Not Nero."

"Well, hell," he said, "that's what makes it

really hard for a dumb carpenter to go out with a smart girl."

She stared at him. "Are we going out?" she whispered.

"No! I just was pointing out more evidence of our incompatibility."

That stung even worse than being called a geek. "At least you got part of it right," she told him.

"Which part? The geek part?"

"I am not a geek!"

He shook his head sadly.

"That line? 'To be or not to be.' It's from a soliloquy in the play *Hamlet*. It's from a scene in the nunnery."

"The nunnery?" he said with satisfaction. "Don't *you* have a fascination?"

"No! You *think* I have a fascination. You are incorrect, just as you are incorrect about me being a geek."

"Yes, and being able to quote Shakespeare, chapter and verse, certainly made that point."

She giggled, and unraveled the fabric from around him.

"Hey! Give me back my toga. I already told you I don't wear underwear!

But it was her turn to play with the gauzy fabric. She inserted herself in the middle of it and twirled until she had made it into a long dress. Then she swathed some around her head, until only her eyes showed. Throwing inhibition to the wind, she swiveled her hips and did some things with her hands.

"Guess who I am?" she purred.

He frowned at her. "A bride?"

The thing he liked least!

"No, I'm not a bride," she snapped.

"A hula girl!"

"No."

"I give up. Stop doing that."

"I'm Mata Hari."

"Who? I asked you to stop."

"Why?"

"It's a little too sexy for the job site."

"A perfect imitation of Mata Hari, then," she said with glee. And she did not stop doing it. She was rather enjoying the look on his face.

"Who?"

"She was a spy. And a dancer."

He burst out laughing as if that was the most improbable thing he had ever heard. "How well versed was she in her Shakespeare?"

"She didn't have to be." Becky began to do a slow writhe with her hips. He didn't seem to think it was funny anymore.

In fact, the ease they had been enjoying—that sense of being a team and working together—evaporated.

He stepped back from her, as if he thought she was going to try kissing him again. She blushed.

"I have so much to do," she squeaked, suddenly feeling silly, and at the very same time, not silly at all.

"Me, too," he said.

But neither of them moved.

"Uh, boss, is this a bad time?"

Mata Hari dropped her veil with a little shriek of embarrassment.

"The guys were thinking maybe we could have a break? It's f—"

Drew stopped his worker with a look.

"It's flipping hot out here. We thought maybe we could go swimming and start again when it's not so hot out."

"Great idea," Drew said. "We all need cooling off, particularly Mata Hari here. You coming swimming, Becky?"

She knew she should say no. She had to say no. She didn't even have a proper bathing suit. Instead she unraveled herself from the yards of fabric, called, "Race you," ran down to the water and flung herself in completely clothed.

Drew's crew crashed into the water around her, following her lead and just jumping in in shorts and T-shirts. They played a raucous game of tag in the water, and she was fully included, though she was very aware of Drew sending out a silent warning that no lines were to be crossed. And none were. It was like having five brothers.

And wouldn't that be the safest thing? Wasn't that what she and Drew had vowed they were going to do? Hadn't they both agreed they were going to retreat into a platonic relationship after the crazy-making sensation of those shared kisses?

What had she been thinking, playing Mata Hari? What kind of craziness was it that she wanted him to not see her exactly as she was: not a spy and dancer who could coax secrets out of unsuspecting men, but a book-loving girl from a small town in America?

After that frolic in the water, the J brothers included her as one of them. Over the next few days, whenever they broke from work to go swimming, one of them came and pounded on her office door and invited her to come.

Today, Josh knocked on the door.

"Swim time," he said.

"I just can't. I have to tie bows on two hundred chairs. And find a cool place to store three thousand potted lavender plants. And—"

Without a word, Josh came in, picked her up and tossed her over his shoulder like a sack of potatoes.

"Stop it. This is my good dress!" She pounded on his back, but of course, with her laughing so hard, he did not take her seriously. She was carried, kicking and screaming and pounding on his back, to the water, where she was unceremoniously dumped in.

"Hey, what the hell are you doing?" Drew demanded, arriving at the water's edge and fishing her out.

The fact that she was screaming with laughter had softened the protective look on his face.

Josh had lifted a big shoulder. "Boss, you said don't take no for an answer."

"No means no, boss," she inserted, barely able to breathe she was laughing so hard.

Drew gave them both an exasperated look, and turned away. Then he turned back, picked her up, raced out into the surf and dumped her again!

She rose from the water sputtering, still holding on to his neck, both their bodies sleek with salt water, her good dress completely ruined.

Gazing into the mischief-filled face of Drew Jordan, Becky was not certain she had ever felt so completely happy.

CHAPTER TWELVE

AFTER THAT BECKY was "in." She and the J's and Drew became a family. They took their meals together and they played together. Becky soon discovered this crew worked hard, and they played harder.

At every break and after work, the football came out. Or the Frisbee. Both games were played with rough-and-tumble delight at the water's edge. She wasn't sure how they could have any energy left, but they did.

The first few times she played, the brothers howled hysterically at both her efforts to throw and catch balls and Frisbees. They good-naturedly nicknamed her Barnside.

"Barnside?" she protested. "That's awful. I demand a new nickname. That is not flattering!"

"You have to earn a new nickname," Jimmy informed her seriously.

"Time to go back to work," Drew told them, after one coffee-break Frisbee session when poor Josh had to climb a palm tree to retrieve a Frisbee she'd thrown. He caught her arm as she turned to leave. "Not you."

"What?" she said.

"Have you heard anything from Allie recently?" he asked.

"The last I heard from her was a few days ago, when she okayed potted lavender instead of tulips." She scanned his face. "You still haven't heard from Joe?"

He shrugged. "It's no big deal."

But she could tell it was. "I'm sorry."

He obviously did not want to talk about his distress over his brother. Becky was aware that she felt disappointed. He was okay with their relationship—with being "friends" on a very light level.

Did he not trust her with his deeper issues?

Apparently not. Drew said, "It's time you learned how to throw a Frisbee. I consider it an essential life skill."

"How could I have missed that?" she asked drily. As much as she wanted to talk to him about his brother, having fun with him was just too tempting. Besides, maybe the lighthearted friendship growing between them would develop some depth, and some trust on his part, if she just gave it time.

"I'm not sure how you could have missed this important life skill," he said, "but it's time to lose 'Barnside.' They are calling you that because you could not hit the side of a barn with a Frisbee at twenty feet."

"At twenty feet? I could!"

"No," Drew informed her with a sad shake of his head, "you couldn't. You've now tossed two Frisbees out to sea, and Josh risked his life to rescue the other one out of the palm tree today. We can't be running out of Frisbees."

"That would be a crisis," she agreed, deadpan.

"I'm glad you understand the seriousness of it. Now, come here."

He placed her in front of him. He gave her a Frisbee. "Don't throw it. Not yet."

He wrapped his arms around her from behind, drawing her back into the powerful support of his chest. He laid his arm along her arm. "It's in the wrist, not the arm. Flick it, don't pitch it." He guided her throw.

Becky actually cackled with delight when it flew true, instead of her normal flub. Soon, he released her to try on her own, and then set up targets for her to throw at. The troubled look that had been on his face since he mentioned his brother evaporated.

Finally, he high-fived her, gave her a little kiss on the nose and headed back to his crew. She watched him go and then looked at the Frisbee in her hand.

How could such a small thing make it feel as if a whole new world was opening up to her? Of course, it wasn't the Frisbee, it was him.

It was being with him and being with his crew.

It occurred to Becky she felt the sense of belonging she had craved since the disintegration of her own family. They were all becoming a team. Drew and his crew were a building machine. The pavilion went up, and they designed and began to build the dance floor. And Becky loved the moments when she and Drew found themselves alone. It was so easy to talk to each other.

The conversation flowed between them so easily. And the laughter.

The hands-off policy had been a good one, even if it was making the tension build almost unbearably between them. It was like going on a diet that had an end date. Not that they had named an end date, but some kind of anticipation was building between them.

And meanwhile, her admiration for him did nothing but grow. He was a natural leader. He was funny. He was smart. She found herself making all kinds of excuses to be around him. She was pretty sure he was doing the same thing to be around her.

The days flew by until there were only three days until the wedding. The details were falling into place seamlessly, not just for the wedding but for the week following. The pagoda and dance floor were done, the wedding gazebo was almost completed, though it still had to be painted.

Usually when she did an event, as the day grew closer her excitement grew, too. But this time she had mixed feelings. In a way, Becky wished the wedding would never come. She had never loved her life as much as she did right now.

Today she was at the helipad looking at the latest shipment of goods. Again, there was a sense of things falling into place: candles in a large box, glass vases for the centerpieces made up of single white roses. She made a note as she instructed the staff member who had been assigned to help her where to put the boxes. Candles would need to be unwrapped and put in candle holders, glass vases cleaned to sparkling. The flowers—accompanied by their own florist—would arrive the evening before the wedding to guarantee freshness.

Then one large, rectangular box with a designer name on it caught her eye. It was the wedding dress. She had not been expecting it. She had assumed it would arrive with Allie.

And yet it made sense that it would need to be hung.

Becky plucked it from all the other boxes and, with some last-minute instructions, walked back to the castle with it. She brought it up to the suite that Allie would inhabit by herself the day before the wedding, and with her new husband after that.

The suite was amazing, so softly romantic it took Becky's breath away. She had a checklist for this room, too. It would be fully supplied with very expensive toiletries, plus fresh flowers would abound. She had chosen the linens from the castle supply room herself.

Becky set the box on the bed. A sticker in red caught her eye. They were instructions stating that the dress should be unpacked, taken out of its plastic protective bag and hung immediately upon arrival. And so Becky opened the box and lifted it out. She unzipped the bag, and carefully lifted the dress out.

Her hands gathered up a sea of white foam. The fabric was silk, so sensuous under her fingertips that Becky could feel the enchantment sewn right into the dress. There was a tall coatrack next to the mirror, and Becky hung the silk-wrapped hanger on a peg and stood back from it.

She could not believe what she was seeing. That long-ago dress that Allie had drawn and given to her, that drawing still living in the back of Becky's dresser drawer, had been brought to life.

The moment was enough to make a girl who had given up on magic believe in it all over again.

Except that's not what it did. Looking at the dress made Becky feel as though she was being stabbed with the shards of her own broken dreams. The dress shimmered with a future she had been robbed of. In every winking pearl, there seemed to be a promise: of someone to share life with, of laughter, of companionship, of passion, of "many babies," fat babies chortling and clapping their hands with glee.

Becky shook herself, as if she was trying to break free of the spell the dress was weaving around her. She wanted to tell herself that she was wrong. That this was not the dress that Allie had drawn on that afternoon of girlish delight all those years ago, not the drawing she had handed to her and said, *This is your wedding dress.*

But she still had that drawing. She had studied it too often now not to know every line of that breathtakingly romantic dress. She had dreamed of herself walking down the aisle in that dress one too many times. There was simply no mistaking which dress it was. Surely, Allie was not being deliberately cruel?

No, Allie had not kept a drawing of the dress. She had given the only existing drawing to Becky. Allie must have remembered it at a subliminal level. Why wouldn't she? The dress was exactly what every single girl dreamed of having one day.

But Becky still felt the tiniest niggle of doubt. What if Drew's cynicism was not misplaced? What if his brother was making a mistake? What if this whole wedding was some kind of publicity stunt orchestrated by Allie? The timing was perfect: Allie was just finishing filming one movie, and another was going to be released in theaters within weeks.

With trembling hands, Becky touched the

fabric of the dress one more time. Then she turned and scurried from the room. She felt as if she was going to burst into tears, as if her every secret hope and dream had been shoved into her face and mocked. And then she bumped right into Drew and did what she least wanted to do. She burst into tears.

"Hey!" Drew eased Becky away from him. She was crying! If there was something worse than her laughing and being joyful and carefree, it was this. "What's the matter?"

"Nothing," she said. "I'm just tired. There's so much to do and—"

But he could tell she wasn't just tired. And from working with her for the past week, he could tell there was hardly anything she liked more than having a lot to do. Her strength was organizing, putting her formidable mind to problems that needed to be solved. No, something had upset her. How had he come to be able to read Becky English so accurately?

She was swiping at those tears, lifting her chin to him with fierce pride, backing away from a shoulder to cry on.

The wisest thing would be to let her. Let her go her own way and have a good cry about whatever, and not involve himself any more than he already had.

Who was he kidding? Just himself. He'd noticed his crew sending him sideways looks every time she was around. He'd noticed Tandu putting them together. He was already involved. Spending the past days with her had cemented that.

"You want to be upset together?" he asked her.

"I told you I'm not upset."

"Uh-huh."

"What are you upset about?"

He lifted a shoulder. "You're not telling, I'm not telling."

"Fine."

"Tandu asked me to give you this."

"How could Tandu have possibly known you were going to bump into me?" Becky asked, taking the paper from him.

"I don't know. The man's spooky. He seems to know things."

Becky squinted at the paper. "Sheesh."

"What?"

"It's a map. He promised it to me over a week ago. Apparently there's a waterfall that would make a great backdrop for wedding pictures. Can you figure out this drawing?"

She handed the map back to him. It looked like a child's map for a pirate's treasure. Drew looked at a big arrow, and the words, *Be careful this rock. Do not fall in water, please.*

"I'll come with you," he decided.

"Thank you," she said. "That's unnecessary." She snatched the map back and looked at it. "Which way is north?"

"I'll come."

The fight went out of her. "Do you ever get tired of being the big brother?"

He thought of how tired he was of leaving Joe messages to call him. He looked at her lips. He thought of how tired he was getting of this friendship between them.

"Suck it up, buttercup," he muttered to himself.

She sighed heavily. "If you have a fault, do you know what it is?"

"Please don't break it to me that I have a fault. Not right now."

"What happened?"

"I said I'm not talking about it, if you're not talking about it."

"Your fault is that you don't answer questions."

"Your fault is—" What was he going to say? Her fault was that she made him think the kind of thoughts he had vowed he was never going to think? "Never mind. Let's go find that waterfall."

"I don't know," Becky said dubiously, after they had been walking twenty minutes. "This seems like kind of a tough walk at any time. I'm in a T-shirt and shorts and I'm overheating. What would it be like in a wedding dress?"

Drew glanced at her. Had she flinched when she said *wedding dress*?

"Maybe her royal highness, the princess Allie is expecting to be delivered to her photo op on a litter carried by two manservants," Drew grumbled. "I hope I'm not going to be one of them."

Becky laughed and took the hand he held back to her to help her scramble over a large boulder.

"Technically, that would be a sedan chair," she said, puffing.

"Huh?"

"A seat that two manservants can carry is sedan chair. Anything bigger is a litter."

He contemplated her. "How do you know this stuff?" he asked.

"That's what a lifetime of reading gets you, a brain teeming with useless information." She contemplated the rock. "Maybe we should just stop here. There's no way Allie can scramble over this rock in a wedding dress."

He contemplated the map. "I think it's only a few more steps. I'm pretty sure I can hear the falls. We might as well see it, even if Allie never will."

And he was right. Only a few steps more and they pushed their way through a gateway of heavy leaves, as big and as wrinkled as elephant ears, and stood in an enchanted grotto.

"Oh, my," Becky breathed.

A frothing fountain of water poured over a twenty-foot cliff and dropped into a pool of pure green water. The pond was surrounded on all sides by lush green ferns and flowers. A large flat rock jutted out into the middle of it, like a platform.

"Perfect for pictures," she thought out loud. "But how are we going to get them here?"

"Wow," Drew said, apparently not the least bit interested in pictures. In a blink, he had stripped off his shirt and dived into the pond. He surfaced and shook his head. Diamonds of water flew. "It's wonderful," he called over the roar of the falls. "Get in."

Once again, there was the small problem of not having bathing attire.

And once again, she was caught in the spell of the island. She didn't care that she didn't have a bathing suit. She wanted to be unencumbered, not just by clothing, but by every single thought that had ever held her prisoner.

CHAPTER THIRTEEN

So AWARE OF the look on Drew's face as he watched her, Becky undid the buttons of her blouse, shrugged it off and then stepped out of her skirt.

When she saw the look on Drew's face, she congratulated herself on her investment in the ultra-sexy and exclusive Rembrandt's Drawing brand underwear. Today, her matching bra and panties were white with tiny red hearts all over them.

And then she stepped into the water. She wanted to dive like him, but because she was not that great a swimmer, she waded in up to her ankles first. The rocks were slipperier than she had expected. Her arms began to windmill.

And she fell, with a wonderful splash, into where he was waiting to catch her.

"The water is fantastic," Becky said, blinking up at him.

"Yes, it is."

She knew neither of them were talking about the water. He set her, it seemed with just a bit of reluctance, on her feet. She splashed him.

"Is that any way to thank me for rescuing you?"

"That is to let you know I did not need to be rescued!"

"Oh," he said. "You planned to fall in the water."

She giggled. "Yes, I did."

"Don't take up poker."

She splashed him again. He got a look on his face. She giggled and bolted away. He was after her in a flash. Soon the grotto was filled with the magic of their splashing and laughter. The days of playing with him—of feeling that sense of belonging—all seemed to have been leading to this. Becky had never felt so free, so wondrous, so aware as she did then.

Finally, exhausted, they hauled themselves out onto the warmth of the large, flat rock, and lay there on their stomachs, side-by-side, panting to catch their breaths.

"I'm indecent," she decided, without a touch of remorse.

"I prefer to think of it as wanton."

She laughed. The sun was coming through

the greenery, dappled on his face. His eyelashes were tangled with water. She laid her hand—wantonly—on the firmness of his naked back. She could feel the warmth of him seeping into her hand. He closed his eyes, as if her touch had soothed something in him. His breathing slowed and deepened.

And then so did hers.

When she awoke, her hand was still on his back. He stirred and opened his eyes, looked at her and smiled.

She shivered with a longing so primal it shook her to the core. Drew's smile disappeared, and he found his feet in one catlike motion. As she sat up and hugged herself, chilled now, he retrieved his T-shirt. He came back and slid it over her head. Then he sat behind her, pulled her between the wedge of his legs and wrapped his arms around her until she stopped shivering.

The light was changing in the grotto and the magic deepened all around them.

"What were you upset about earlier?" he asked softly.

She sighed. "I unpacked Allie's wedding dress."

He sucked in his breath. "And what? You wished it was yours?"

"It was mine," she whispered. "It was the dress she drew for me one of those afternoons all those years ago."

"What? The very same dress? Maybe you're just remembering it wrong."

Was there any way to tell him she had kept that picture without seeming hopelessly pathetic?

"No," she said firmly. "It was that dress."

"Representing all your hopes and dreams," he said. "No wonder you were crying."

She felt a surge of tenderness for him that there was no mockery in his tone, but instead, a lovely empathy.

"It was just a shock. I am hoping it is just a weird coincidence. But I'm worried. I didn't know Allie that well when we were teenagers. I don't know her at all now. What if it's all some gigantic game? What if she's playing with everyone?"

"Exactly the same thing I was upset about," Drew confessed to her. "My brother was supposed to be here. He's not. I've called him twice a day, every day, since I got here to find out why. He won't return my calls. That isn't like him."

"Tell me what *is* like him," Becky said gently.

And suddenly he just wanted to unburden

himself. He felt as if he had carried it all alone for so long, and he was not sure he could go one more step with the weight of it all. It felt as if it was crushing him.

He was not sure he had ever felt this relaxed or this at ease with another person. Drew had a deep sense of being able to trust this woman in front of him. It felt as if every day before this one—all those laughter-filled days of getting to know one another, of splashing and playing, and throwing Frisbees—had been leading to this.

He needed to think about that: that this wholesome woman, with her girl-next-door look, was really a Mata Hari, a temptress who could pull secrets from an unwilling man. But he didn't heed the warning that was flashing in the back of his brain like a red light telling of a train coming.

Drew just started to talk, and it felt as if a rock had been removed from a dam that had held back tons of water for years. Now it was all flowing toward that opening, trying to get out.

"When my parents died, I was seventeen. I wasn't even a mature seventeen. I was a superficial surfer dude, riding a wave through life."

Something happened to Becky's face. A

softness came to it that was so real it almost stole the breath out of his chest. It was so different than the puffy-lipped coos of sympathy that he had received from women in the past when he'd made the mistake of sharing even small parts of his story.

This felt as if he could go lay his head on Becky's slender, naked shoulder, and rest there for a long, long time.

"I'm so sorry," she said quietly, "about the death of your parents. Both of them died at the same time?"

"It was a car accident." He could stop right there, but no, he just kept going. All those words he had never spoken felt as if they were now rushing to escape a building on fire, jostling with each other in their eagerness to be out.

"They had gone out to celebrate the anniversary of some friends. They never came home. A policeman arrived at the door and told me what had happened. Not their fault at all, a drunk driver…"

"Drew," she breathed softly. Somehow her hand found his, and the dam within him was even more compromised.

"You have never met a person more totally

unqualified for the job of raising a seven-year-old brother than the seventeen-year-old me."

She squeezed his hand, as if she believed in the younger him, making him want to go on, to somehow dissuade this faith in him.

He cleared his throat. "It was me or foster care, so—" He rolled his shoulders.

"I think that's the bravest thing I ever heard," she said.

"No, it wasn't," he said fiercely. "Brave is when you have a choice. I didn't have any choice."

"You did," she insisted, as fierce as him. "You did have a choice and you chose love."

That word inserted into any conversation between them should have stopped it cold. But it didn't. In fact, it felt as if more of the wall around everything he held inside crumbled, as if her words were a wrecking ball seeking the weakest point in that dam.

"I love my brother," he said. "I just don't know if he knows how much I do."

"He can't be that big a fool," Becky said.

"I managed to finish out my year in high school and then I found a job on a construction crew. I was tired all the time. And I never seemed to be able to make enough money. Joe sure wasn't wearing the designer clothes the rest of the kids had. I got mad if he asked. That's why he probably doesn't have a clue how I feel about him."

Becky's hand was squeezing his with unbelievable strength. It was as if her strength—who could have ever guessed this tiny woman beside him held so much strength?—was passing between them, right through the skin of her hand into his, entering his bloodstream.

"I put one foot in front of the other," Drew told her. "I did my best to raise my brother. But I was so scared of messing up that I think I was way too strict with him. I thought if I let him know how much I cared about him he would perceive it as weakness and I would lose control. Of him. Of life.

"I'd already seen what happened when I was not in control."

"Did you feel responsible for the death of your parents?" she asked. He could hear that she was startled by the question.

"I guess I asked myself, over and over, what I could have done. And the answer seemed to be, 'Never let anyone you love out of your sight. Never let go.' Most days, I felt as if I was hanging on by a thread.

"When he was a teen? I was not affectionate. I was like Genghis Khan, riding roughshod over the troops. The default answer to almost everything he wanted to do was *no*. When I did loosen the reins a bit, he had to check in with me. He had a curfew. I sucked, and he let me know it."

"Sucked?" she said, indignant.

"Yeah, we both agreed on that. Not that I let him know I agreed with him in the you-suck department."

"Then you were both wrong. What you did was noble," she said quietly. "The fact that you think you did it imperfectly does not make it less noble."

"Noble!" he snapped, wanting to show only annoyance and not vulnerability. "There's nothing noble about acting on necessity."

But she was having none of it. "It's even noble that you saw it as a necessity, not a choice."

"Whatever," he said. He suddenly disliked himself. He felt as if he was a small dog yapping and yapping and yapping at the postman. He sat up. She sat up, too. He folded his arms over his chest, a shield.

"Given that early struggle, you seem to have done well for yourself."

"A man I worked for gave me a break," Drew admitted, even though he had ordered himself to stop talking. "He was a developer. He told me I could have a lot in one of his subdivisions and put up a house on spec. I didn't have to pay for the lot until the house sold. It was the beginning of an amazing journey, but looking back, I think my drive to succeed also made me emotionally unavailable to my brother."

"You feel totally responsible for him, still."

Drew sighed, dragged a hand through his sun-dried hair. "I'm sure it's because of how I raised him that we are in this predicament we're in now, him marrying a girl I know nothing about, who may be using him. And you. And all of us."

"I don't see that as your fault."

"If I worked my ass off, I could feed him," he heard himself volunteering. "I could keep the roof over his head. I could get his books for school. I even managed to get him through college. But—"

"But what?"

"I could not teach him about finding a good relationship." Drew's voice dropped to a hoarse whisper. It felt as if every single word he had said had been circling around this essential truth.

"I missed them so much, my mom and dad. They could have showed him what he should be looking for. They were so stable. My mom was a teacher, my dad was a postal worker. Ordinary people, and yet they elevated the ordinary.

"I didn't know what I had when I had it. I didn't know what it was to wake up to my dad downstairs, making coffee for my mom, delivering it to her every morning. He sang a song while he delivered it. An old Irish folk song. They were always laughing and teasing each other. We were never rich but our house was full. The smell of cookies, the sound of them arguing good-naturedly about where to put the Christmas tree, my mom reading stories. I loved those stories way after I was too old for them. I used to find some excuse to hang out when she was reading to Joe at night. How could I hope to give any of that kind of love to my poor orphaned baby brother? When even thinking about all we had lost felt as if it would undermine the little bit of control that I was holding over my world? Instead, the environment I raised Joe in was so devoid of affection that he's gotten involved with Allie out of his sheer desperation to be loved."

"Maybe he longs for your family as much as you do."

"It's not that I didn't love him," Drew admitted gruffly. "I just didn't know how to say that to him."

"Maybe that's the area where he's going to teach you," she said softly.

Something shivered up and down Drew's spine, a tingle of pure warning, like a man might feel seconds before the cougar pounced from behind, or the plane began to lose altitude, or the earth began to shake. The remainder of the dam wall felt as if it tumbled down inside him.

"You can say that, even after finding the dress? When neither of us is sure about Allie or what her true motives are?"

"I'm going to make a decision to believe love is going to win. No matter what."

He stared at her. There should have been a choice involved here. There should have been a choice to get up and run.

But if there was that choice? He was helpless to make it.

Instead he went into her open arms like a warrior who had fought too many battles, like a warrior who had thought he would never see the lights of familiar fires again. He laid his head upon her breast and felt her hand, tender, on the nape of his neck.

He sighed against her, like a warrior who

unexpectedly found himself in the place he had given up on. That place was home.

"You did your best," she said softly. "You can forgive yourself if you weren't perfect."

She began to hum softly. And then she began to sing. Her voice was clear and beautiful and it raised the hair on the back of his neck. It was as if it affirmed that love was the greatest force of all, and that it survived everything, even death.

Because of the millions of songs in the world, how was it possible Becky was gently singing this one, in her soft, true voice?

It was the same song his father had sung to his mother, every day as he brought her coffee.

Drew's surrender was complete. He had thought his story spilling out of him, like water out of a dam that had been compromised, would make him feel weak, and as though he had lost control.

Instead, he felt connected to Becky in a way he had not allowed himself to feel connected to another human being in a long, long time.

Instead, he realized how alone he had been in the world, and how good it felt not to be alone.

Instead, listening to her voice soar above the roar of the waterfall and feeling it tingle along his spine, it felt as though the ice was melting from around his heart. He felt the way he had felt diving into the water to save her all those days ago. He felt brave. Only this time, he felt as if he might be saving himself.

Drew realized he felt as brave as he ever had. He contemplated the irony that a complete surrender would make him feel the depth of his own courage.

You heal now.

And impossibly, beautifully, he was.

CHAPTER FOURTEEN

NIGHT HAD FALLEN by the time they left the waterfall and found their way back to the castle grounds. He left her with his T-shirt and walked beside her bare-chested, happy to give her the small protection of his clothing. He walked her to her bedroom door, and they stood there, looking at each other, drinking each other in like people who had been dying of thirst and had found a spring.

He touched the plumpness of her lip with his thumb, and her tongue darted out and tasted him.

She sighed her surrender, and he made a guttural, groaning sound of pure need. He did what he had been wanting to do all this time.

He planted his hands, tenderly, on either side of her head, and dropped his lips over hers. He kissed her thoroughly, exploring the tenderness of her lips with his own lips, and his tongue, probing the cool grotto of her mouth.

He had thought Becky, his little bookworm, would be shy, but she had always had that surprising side, and she surprised him now.

That gentle kiss of recognition, of welcome, that sigh of surrender, deepened quickly into something else.

It was need and it was desire. It was passion and it was hunger. It was nature singing its ancient song of wanting life to have victory over the cycle of death.

That was what was in this kiss: everything it was to be human. Instinct and intuition, power and surrender, pleasure that bordered on pain it was so intense. He dragged his lips from hers and anointed her earlobes and her eyelids, her cheeks and the tip of her nose. He kissed the hollow of her throat, and then she pulled him back to her lips.

Her hands were all over him, touching, exploring, celebrating the hard strength in the muscles that gloried at the touch of her questing fingertips.

Finally, rational thought pushed through his primal reaction to her, calling a stern *no*. But it took every ounce of Drew's substantial strength to peel back from her. She stood there, quivering with need, panting, her eyes wide on his face.

His rational mind was gaining a foothold now that he had managed to step back from her. She had never looked more beautiful, even though her hair was a mess, and any makeup she had been wearing had washed off long ago. She had never looked more beautiful, even though she was standing there in a T-shirt that was way too large for her.

But nothing could hide the light shining from her. It was the purity of that light that reminded Drew that Becky was not the kind of girl you tangled with lightly. She required his intentions to be very clear.

In the past few days, he had felt his mother's spirit around him in a way he had not experienced since her death. It was the kind of idea he might have scoffed at two short weeks ago.

And yet this island, with its magic, and Becky with her own enchantment, made things that had seemed impossible before feel entirely possible now.

Drew knew his mother would be expecting him to be a decent man, expecting him to rise to what she would have wanted him to be if she had lived.

She knew what he had forgotten about himself: that he was a man of courage and decency.

Drew took another step back from Becky. He saw the sense of loss and confusion in her face.

"I have to go," he said, his voice hoarse.

"Please, don't."

Her voice was hoarse, too, and she stepped toward him. She took the waistband of his shorts and pulled her to him with surprising strength.

"Don't go," she said fiercely.

"You don't know what you're asking."

"Yes, I do."

For a moment he was so torn, but then his need to be decent won out. If things were going to go places with this girl—and he knew they were—it would require him to be a better man than he had been with women in the past.

It would require him to do the honorable thing.

"I have to make a phone call tonight, before it's too late." It was a poor excuse, but it was the only one he could think of. With great reluctance, he untangled her hands from where they held him, and once again stepped back from her.

If she asked again, he was not going to be able to refuse. A man's strengths had limits, after all.

But she accepted his decision. She raked a

hand through her hair and looked disgruntled, but pulled herself together and tilted her chin at him.

"I have a phone call to make, too," she said. She was, just like that, his little bookworm spelling-bee contestant again, prim and sensible, and pulling back from the wild side she had just shown him.

She took a step back from him.

Go, he ordered himself. But he didn't. He stepped back toward her. He kissed her again, quickly, and then he tore himself away from her and went to his own quarters.

Rattled by what he was feeling, he took a deep breath. He wandered to the window and looked at the moon, and listened to the lap of the water on the beach. He felt as alive as he had ever felt.

He glanced at the time, swore softly, took out his cell phone and stabbed in Joe's number.

There was, predictably, no answer. He needed to tell Joe what he had learned of love tonight. It might save Joe from imminent disaster. But, of course, there was no answer, and you could hardly leave a message saying somehow you had stumbled on the secret of life and you needed to share that *right now*.

Joe would think his coolheaded, hard-hearted

brother had lost his mind. So, that conversation would have to wait until tomorrow.

According to the information Becky had, Joe and Allie were supposed to arrive only on the morning of the wedding day. This was apparently to slip under the radar of the press.

Tomorrow, the guests would begin arriving, in a coordinated effort that involved planes and boats landing on Sainte Simone all day.

Two hundred people. It was going to be controlled chaos. And then Joe and Allie would arrive the next day, just hours before the wedding. How was he going to get Joe alone? Drew was aware that he *had* to get his brother alone, that he *had* to figure out what the hell was really going on between him and Allie.

And he was aware that he absolutely *had* to protect Becky. He thought of her tears over that dress that Allie had had specially made, and he felt fury building in him. In fact, all the fury of his powerlessness over Joe's situation seemed to be coming to a head.

"Look, Joe," he said, after that annoying beep that made him want to pick up the chair beside his bed and throw it against the wall, "I don't know what your fiancée is up to, but you give her a message from me. You tell your betrothed if she does anything to hurt Becky

English—anything—I will not rest until I've tracked her to the ends of the earth and dealt with it. You know me well enough to know I mean it. I'm done begging you to call me. But I don't think you have a clue what you're getting mixed up in."

Drew disconnected the call, annoyed with himself. He had lost control, and probably reduced his chances of getting his brother to meet with him alone.

Becky went to her room and shut the door, leaning against it. Her knees felt wobbly. She felt breathless. She touched her lips, as if she could still feel the warmth of his fire claiming her. She hugged herself. She could not believe she had invited Drew Jordan into her room. She was not that kind of girl!

Thank goodness his good sense had prevailed, but what did that mean? That he was not feeling things quite as intensely as she was?

She sank down on her bed. It was as if the world had gone completely silent, and into that silence flowed a frightening truth.

She had fallen for Drew Jordan. She loved him. She had never felt anything like what she was feeling right now: tingling with aliveness, excited about the future, aware that life had the potential to hold the most miraculous surprises. She, Becky English, who had sworn off it, had still fallen under its spell. She was in love. It wasn't just the seduction of this wildly romantic setting. It wasn't.

She loved him so much.

It didn't make any sense. It was too quick, wasn't it?

But, in retrospect, her relationship with Jerry had made perfect sense, and had unfolded with respectable slowness.

And there had been nothing real about it. She had been chasing security. She had settled for safety. Salt and pepper. Good grief, she had almost made herself a prisoner of a dull and ordinary life.

But now she knew how life was supposed to feel. And she felt so alive and grateful and on fire with all the potential the days ahead held. They didn't feel safe at all. They felt like they were loaded with unpredictable forces and choices. It felt as if she was plunging into the great unknown, and she was astonished to find she *loved* how the great adventure that was life and love was making her feel.

And following on the heels of her awareness of how much she loved Drew, and how much that love was going to make her life change, Becky felt a sudden fury with his brother. How could he treat Drew like this? Surely Joe was not so stupid that he could not see his brother had sacrificed everything for him? Drew's whole life had become about making a life for his brother, about holding everything together. He had tried so hard and done so much, and now Joe would not even return his phone calls?

It was wrong. It was just plain old wrong.

Becky's fingers were shaking when she dialed Allie's number. She didn't care that it was late in Spain. She didn't care at all. Of course, after six rings she got Allie's voice commanding her to leave a message.

"Allie, it's Becky English. I need you to get an urgent message to Joe. He needs to call his brother. He needs to call Drew right now. Tomorrow morning at the latest." There, that was good enough. But her voice went on, shaking with emotion. "It's unconscionable that he would be ignoring Drew's attempts to call him after all Drew has done for him. I know you will both be arriving here early on the morning of the wedding, but he needs to talk to Drew before that. As soon as you get this message he needs to call."

There. She didn't need to say one other thing. And yet somehow she was still talking.

"You tell him if he doesn't call his brother immediately he'll be…" She thought and then said, "Dealing with me!"

She disconnected her phone. Then snickered. She had just used a terrible, demanding tone of voice on the most prosperous client she had ever had. She didn't care. What was so funny was her saying Drew's brother would be dealing with her, as if that was any kind of threat.

And yet she felt more powerful right now than she had ever felt in her entire life. It did feel as if she could whip that disrespectful young pup into shape!

That's what love did, she supposed. It didn't take away power, it gave it.

Becky allowed herself to feel the shock of that. She had somehow, someway, fallen in love with Drew Jordan. And not just a little bit in love: irrevocably, crazily, impossibly, feverishly in love.

It was nothing at all like what she had thought was love with Jerry. Nothing. That had felt safe and solid and secure, even though it had turned out to be none of those things. This was the most exciting thing that she had ever felt. It felt as if she was on the very crest of the world's highest roller coaster, waiting for that stomach-dropping swoop downward, her heart in her throat, both terrified and exhilarated by the pathway ahead. And just like that roller coaster, it felt as if somehow she had fully committed before she knew exactly where it was all leading. It felt like now she had no choice but to hang on tight and enjoy the wildest ride of her life.

In a trance of delight at the unexpected turn in her life, Becky pulled off Drew's T-shirt and put on her pajamas. And then she rolled up the T-shirt, and even though it was still slightly damp, she used it as her pillow and drifted off to sleep with the scent of him lulling her like a boat rocking on gentle waves.

She awoke the next morning to the steady *wop-wop-wop* of helicopter blades slicing the air. At first, she lay in bed, hugging Drew's T-shirt, listening and feeling content. Waking up to the sound of helicopters was not unusual on Sainte Simone. It was the primary way that supplies were delivered, and with the wedding just one day away, all kinds of things would be arriving today. Fresh flowers. The cake. The photographer.

Two hundred people would also be arriving over the course of the day, on boats and by small commercial jets.

There was no time for lollygagging, Becky told herself sternly. She cast back the covers, gave the T-shirt one final hug before putting it under her pillow and then got up and went to the window.

One day, she thought, looking at the helicopters buzzing above her. She had to focus. She had to shake off this dazed, delicious feeling that she was in love and that was all that mattered.

And then it slowly penetrated her bliss that something was amiss. Her mouth fell open. She should have realized from the noise levels that something was dreadfully wrong, but she had not.

There was not one helicopter in the skies above Sainte Simone. From her place at the window, she could count half a dozen. It looked like an invasion force, but with none of the helicopters even attempting to land. They were hovering and dipping and swooping.

She could see a cameraman leaning precariously out one open door! There were so many helicopters in the tiny patch of sky above the island that it was amazing they were managing not to crash into each other.

As she watched, one of the aircraft swooped down over the pavilion. The beautiful white gauze panels began to whip around as though they had been caught in a hurricane. One ripped away, and was swept on air currents out to the ocean, where it floated down in the water, looking for all the world like a bridal veil.

A man—Josh, she thought—raced out into the surf and grabbed the fabric, then shook his fist at the helicopter. The helicopter swooped toward him, the cameraman leaning way out to get that shot.

Becky turned from the window, got dressed quickly and hurried down the stairs and out the main door onto the lawn. The staff were all out there—even the chef in his tall hat—staring in amazement at the frenzied sky dance above them.

Josh came and thrust the wet ball of fabric at her.

"Sorry," he muttered. Tandu turned and looked at her sadly. "It's on the news this morning. That the wedding is here, tomorrow. I have satellite. It's on every single channel."

She felt Drew's presence before she saw him. She felt him walk up beside her and she turned to him, and scanned his familiar face, wanting him to show her how to handle this and what to do.

He put his hand on her shoulder, and she nestled into the weight of it. This is what it meant to not be alone. Life could throw things at you, but you didn't have to handle it all by yourself. The weight of the catastrophe could be divided between them.

Couldn't it? She turned to him. "What are we going to do?"

He looked at her blankly, and she realized he was trying to read her lips. There was no way he could have heard her. She repeated her question, louder.

"I don't know," he said.

He didn't know? She felt a faint shiver of disappointment.

"How could we hold a wedding under these circumstances?" she shouted. "No one will be able to hear anything. The fabric is already tearing away from the pavilion. What about Allie's dress? And veil? What about dinner and candles and…" Her voice fell away.

"I don't think there's going to be a wedding," he said.

Her sense of her whole world shifting intensified. He could not save the day. Believing that he could would only lead to disillusionment. Believing in another person could only lead to heartache.

How on earth had she been so swept away that she had forgotten that?

She shot him a look. He sounded sorry, but was there something else in his voice? She studied Drew more carefully. He had his handsome head tilted to look at the helicopters, his arms folded over his chest.

Did he look grimly satisfied that there was a very good possibility that there was going to be no wedding?

CHAPTER FIFTEEN

BECKY FELT HER heart plummet, and it was not totally because the wedding she had worked so hard on now seemed to be in serious danger of being canceled.

Who, more than any other person on the face of the earth, did not want this wedding to happen?

Drew took his eyes from the sky and looked at her. He frowned. "Why are you looking at me like that?"

"I was just wondering about that phone call you were all fired up to make last night," she said. She could hear the stiffness in her own voice, and she saw that her tone registered with him.

"I recall being all fired up," he said, "but not about a phone call."

How dare he throw that in her face right now? That she had invited him in. He saw it as being all fired up. She saw, foolishly, that she had put her absolute trust in him.

"Is this why you didn't come in?" she said, trying to keep her tone low and be heard above the helicopters at the same time.

"Say what?"

"You didn't give in to my wanton invitation because you already knew you were planning this, didn't you?"

"Planning this?" he echoed, his brow furrowing. "Planning what, exactly?"

Becky sucked in a deep breath. "You let it out, didn't you?"

"What?"

"Don't play the innocent with me! You let it out on purpose, to stop the wedding. To stop your brother and Allie from getting married, to buy yourself a little more time to convince him not to do it."

He didn't deny it. Something glittered in his eyes, hard and cold, that she had never seen before. She reminded herself, bitterly, that there were many things about him she had never seen before. She had only known him two weeks. How could she, who of all people should be well versed in the treachery of the human heart, have let her guard down?

"That's why you had to rush to the phone

last night," she decided. "Maybe you even thought you were protecting me. I should have never told you about the wedding dress."

"There are a lot of things we should have never told each other," he bit out.

She stared at him and realized the awful truth. It had all happened too fast between them. It was a reminder to her that they didn't know each other at all. She had been susceptible to the whole notion of love. Because the island was so romantic, because of that dress, because of those crazy moments when she had wanted to feel unencumbered, she had thrown herself on the altar of love with reckless abandon.

She'd been unencumbered all right! Every ounce of good sense she'd possessed had fled her!

But really, hadn't she known this all along? That love was that roller coaster ride, thrilling and dangerous? And that every now and then it went right off the tracks?

She shot him an accusing look. He met her gaze unflinchingly.

A plane circled overhead and began to prepare to land through the minefield of helicopters. Over his shoulder, she could see a passenger barge plowing through seas made rough by the wind coming off those blades.

"Guess what?" she said wearily. "That will be the first of the guests arriving. All those people are expecting a wedding."

He lifted a shoulder negligently. What all those people were expecting didn't matter one iota to him. And neither did all her hard work. Or what this disaster could mean to her career. He didn't care about her at all.

But if he thought she was going to take this lying down, he was mistaken.

"I'm going to call Allie's publicity people," she said, with fierce determination. "Maybe they can make this disaster stop. Maybe they can call off the hounds if they are offered something in exchange."

"Good luck with that," Drew said coolly. "My experience with hounds, limited as it might be, is once they've caught the scent, there is no calling them off."

"I'm sure if Allie offers to do a photo shoot just for them, after the wedding, they will stop this. I'm sure of it!"

Of course, she was no such thing.

He gazed at her. "Forever hopeful," he said. She heard the coldness in his tone, as if being hopeful was a bad thing.

And it was! She had allowed herself to hope she could love this man. And now she saw it was impossible. Now, when it was too late. When she could have none of the glory and all of the pain.

Drew could not let Becky see how her words hit him, like a sword cleaving him in two. Last night he had taken the biggest chance he had ever taken. He had trusted her with everything. He had been wide-open.

Love.

Sheesh. He, of all people, should know better than that. Joe had not called him back. That's what love really was. Leaving yourself wide-open, all right, wide-open to pain. And rejection. Leaving yourself open to the fact that the people you loved most of all could misinterpret everything you did, run it through their own filter and come to their own conclusions, as wrong as those might be. He, of all people, should know that better than anyone else.

How could she think that he would do this to her? How could she trust him so little? He felt furious with her, and fury felt safe. Because when his fury with Becky died down, he knew what would remain. What always remained when love was gone. Pain. An emptiness so vast it felt as though it could swallow a man whole.

And he, knowing that truth as intimately as any man could know it, had still left himself wide-open to revisiting that pain. What did that mean?

"That I'm stupid," he told himself nastily. "Just plain old garden-variety stupid."

Becky felt as if she was in a trance. Numb. But it didn't matter what she was feeling. She'd agreed to do a job, and right now her job was welcoming the first of the wedding guests to the island and trying to hide it from them all that the wedding of the century was quickly turning into the fiasco of the century.

She stood with a smile fixed on her face as the door of the plane opened and the first passenger stepped down onto the steps.

In a large purple hat, and a larger purple dress, was Mrs. Barchkin, her now retired high school social sciences teacher.

"Why, Becky English!" Mrs. Barchkin said cheerily. "What on earth are you doing here?"

Her orders had been to keep the wedding secret. She had not told one person in her small town she was coming here.

Her smile clenched in place, she said, "No, what on earth are you doing here?"

Mrs. Barchkin was clutching a rumpled card in a sweaty hand. She passed it to Becky. Despite the fact people were piling up behind Mrs. Barchkin, Becky smoothed out the card and read, "In appreciation of your kindness, I ask you to be my guest at a celebration of love." There were all the details promising a limousine pickup and the adventure of a lifetime.

"Pack for a week and plan to have fun!" And all this was followed with Allie Ambrosia's flowing signature, both the small *i*'s dotted with hearts.

"Isn't this all too exciting?" Mrs. Barchkin said.

"Too exciting," Becky agreed woodenly. "If you just go over there, that golf cart will take you to your accommodations. Don't worry about your luggage."

Don't worry. Such good advice. But Becky's sense of worry grew as she greeted the rest of the guests coming down the steps of the plane. There was a poor-looking young woman in a cheaply made dress, holding a baby who looked ill. There was a man and a wife and their three kids chattering about the excitement of their first plane ride. There was a minister. At least he *might* be here to conduct the ceremony.

Not a single passenger who got off that plane was what you would expect of Hollywood's A-list. And neither, Becky realized an hour later, was anyone who got off the passenger barge. In fact, most everyone seemed to be the most ordinary of people, people who would have fit right in on Main Street in Moose Run.

They were all awed by the island and the unexpected delight of an invitation to the wedding of one of the most famous people in the world. But none of them—not a single person of the dozens that were now descending on the island—actually seem to know Allie Ambrosia or Joe Jordan.

Becky had a deepening conviction that somehow they were all pawns in Allie's big game. Maybe, just maybe, Drew had not been so wrong in doing everything he could to stop the wedding.

But why had he played with her? Why had he made it seem as if he was going along with getting a wedding ready if he was going to sabotage it? Probably, this—the never-ending storm of helicopters hovering overhead—had been a last-ditch effort to stop things when his every effort to reach his brother had been frustrated.

Still, the fact was she had trusted him. She was not going to make excuses for him! She was determined to not even think about him.

As each boat and plane delivered its guests and departed, Becky's unease grew. Her increasingly frantic texts and messages to Allie and members of Allie's staff were not being answered. In fact, Allie's voice mailbox was now full.

Becky crawled into bed that night, exhausted. The wedding was less than twenty-four hours away. If they were going to cancel it, they needed to do that now.

Though one good thing about all the excitement was that she had not had time to give a thought to Drew. But now she did.

And lying there in her bed, staring at the ceiling, she burst into tears. And the next morning she was thankful she had used up every one of her tears, because a private jet landed at precisely 7:00 a.m.

The door opened.

And absolutely nothing happened. Eventually, the crew got off. A steward told her, cheerfully, they were going to layover here. He showed her the same invitation she had seen at least a dozen times. The one that read, "In appreciation of your kindness, I ask you to be my guest at a celebration of love."

Becky had to resist the impulse to tear that invitation from his hands and rip it into a million pieces. Because now she knew the plane was empty. And Allie and Joe had not gotten off it.

Of course, it could be part of the elaborate subterfuge that was necessary to avoid the paparazzi, but the helicopters overhead were plenty of evidence they had already failed at that.

How could she, Becky asked herself with a shake of her head, still hope? How could she still hope they were coming, and still hope that love really was worth celebrating?

She quit resisting the impulse. She took the invitation from the crew member, tore it into a dozen pieces and threw them to the wind. Despite the surprised looks she received, it felt amazingly good to do that!

She turned and walked away. No more hoping. No more trying to fill in the blanks with optimistic fiction. She was going to have to find Tandu and cancel everything. She was going to have to figure out the logistics of how to get all those disappointed people back out of here.

Her head hurt thinking about it.

So Drew had won the headache competition after all. And by a country mile at that.

CHAPTER SIXTEEN

DREW PULLED HIMSELF from the ocean and flung himself onto the beach. His crew had just finished the gazebo and had departed, sending him looks that let him know he'd been way too hard on them. He'd had them up at dawn, putting the final touches of paint on the gazebo, making sure the dance floor was ready.

What did they expect? There was supposed to be a wedding here in a few hours. Of course he had been hard on them.

Maybe a little too hard, since it now seemed almost everyone on the island, except maybe the happy guests, had figured out the bride and groom were missing.

Drew knew his foul mood had nothing to do with the missing bride and groom, or the possibility, growing more real by the second, that there wasn't going to be a wedding. He had driven his crew to perfection anyway, unreasonably.

He had tried to swim it off, but now, lying in the sand, he was aware he had not. The helicopter that buzzed him to see if he was anyone interesting did not help his extremely foul mood.

How could Becky possibly think he had called the press? After all they had shared together, how could she not know who he really was?

It penetrated his morose that his phone, lying underneath his shirt, up the beach, was ringing. And then he froze. The ring tone was the one he had assigned for Joe!

He got up and sprinted across the sand.

"Hello?"

"Hi, bro."

It felt like a shock to hear his brother's voice. Even in those two small syllables, Drew was sure he detected something. Sheepishness?

"How are you, Drew?"

"Cut the crap."

Silence. He thought Joe might have hung up on him, but he heard him breathing.

"Where the hell have you been? Why haven't you been answering my calls? Are you on your way here?"

"Drew, I have something to tell you."

Drew was aware he was holding his breath.

"Allie and I got married an hour ago."

"What?"

"The whole island thing was just a ruse. Allie leaked it to the press yesterday morning that we were going to get married there to divert them away from where we really are."

"You lied to me?" He could hear the disbelief and disappointment in his own voice.

"I feel terrible about that. I'm sorry."

"But why?"

Inside he was thinking, *How could you get married without me to stand beside you? I might have made mistakes, but I'm the one who has your back. Who has always had your back.*

"It's complicated," Joe said.

"Let me get this straight. You aren't coming here at all?"

"No."

Poor Allie, Drew thought.

"We got married an hour ago, just Allie and me and a justice of the peace. We're in Topeka, Kansas. Who would ever think to look there, huh?"

"Topeka, Kansas," he repeated dully.

His brother took it as a question. "You don't have to be a resident of the state to get married here. There's a three-day waiting period for the license, but I went down and applied for it a month ago."

"You've been planning this for a month?" Drew felt the pain of it. He had been excluded from one of the most important events of his brother's life. And it was his own fault.

"I'm sorry," he said.

"For what?" Joe sounded astounded.

"That I could never tell you what you needed to hear."

"I'm not following."

"That I loved you and cared about you and would have fought alligators for you."

"Drew! You think I don't know that?"

"I guess if you know it, I don't understand any of this."

"It's kind of all part of a larger plan. I'll fill you in soon. I promise. Meanwhile, Allie's got her people on it right now. In a few hours the press will know we aren't there, and whatever's going on there will die down. They'll leave you guys alone."

"Leave us alone? You think I'm going to stay here?"

"Why not? It's a party. That's all the invitations ever said. That it was a party to celebrate love."

"Who are all these people arriving here?"

And when Joe told him, Drew could feel himself, ever so reluctantly, letting go of the anger.

Even his anger at Becky felt as if it was dissipating.

He understood, suddenly, exactly why she had jumped at the first opportunity to see him in a bad light. That girl was terrified of love. She'd been betrayed by it at too many turns. She was terrified of what she was feeling for him.

"Joe? Tell Allie not to call Becky about the wedding not happening. I'll look after it. I'll tell her myself."

There was a long silence. And then Joe said softly, "All part of a larger plan."

"Yeah, whatever." He wanted to tell his brother congratulations, but somehow he couldn't. Who was this woman that Joe had married? It seemed as if she was just playing with all their strings as if they were her puppets.

Drew threw on his shirt and took the now familiar path back toward the castle. What remained of his anger at Becky for not trusting him was completely gone.

All he wanted to do was protect her from

one more devastating betrayal. He understood, suddenly, what love was. With startling clarity he saw that it was the ability to see that it was not all about him. To be able to put her needs ahead of his own and not be a baby because his feelings had been hurt.

As he got closer to the castle, he could see there were awestruck people everywhere prowling the grounds. He spotted Tandu in the crowd, talking to a tall, distinguished-looking man in a casual white suit and bare feet.

"Mr. Drew Jordan, have you met Mr. Lung?" Tandu asked him.

"Pleasure," Drew said absently. "Tandu, can I talk to you for a minute?"

Tandu stepped to the side with him. "Have you seen Becky?" he asked, with some urgency.

"A few minutes ago. She told me to cancel everything."

So, she already knew, or thought she did. She was carrying the burden of it by herself.

"Impossible to cancel," Tandu said. "The wedding must go on!"

"Tandu, there is not going to be a wedding. I just spoke to my brother."

"Ah," he said. "Oh, well, we celebrate love anyway, hmm?" And then he gave Drew a look that was particularly piercing, and disappeared into the crowd.

"How are you enjoying my island?" Bart Lung was on his elbow.

"It's a beautiful place," Drew said, scanning the crowd for Becky. "Uh, look, Mr. Lung—"

"Bart, please."

"Bart, I think you need to have a qualified first aid person on the island to host this many guests."

"I have an excellent first aid attendant. That was him who just introduced us. Don't be fooled by the tray of canapés."

"Look, Tandu is a nice guy. Stellar. I just don't think being afraid of blood is a great trait for a first aid attendant."

"Tandu? Afraid of blood? Who told you that?"

Before Drew could answer that Tandu himself had told him that, Bart went on.

"Tandu is from this island, but don't be fooled by that island boy accent or the white shirt or the tray of canapés. He's a medical student at Oxford. He comes back in the summers to help out." Bart chortled. "Afraid of blood! I saw him once when he was the first responder to a shark attack. I have never seen so much blood and I have never seen such cool under pressure."

Drew felt a shiver run up and down the whole length of his spine.

And then he saw Becky. She was talking to someone who was obviously a member of the flight crew, and she was waving her arms around expressively.

"Excuse me. I have an urgent matter I need to take care of."

"Of course."

"Becky!"

She turned and looked at him, and for a moment, everything she felt was naked in her face.

And everything she was.

Drew realized fully that her lack of trust was a legacy from her past, and that to be the man she needed, the man worthy of her love, he needed to not hurt her more, but to understand her fears and vulnerabilities and to help her heal them.

Just as she had, without even knowing that was what she was doing, helped him heal his own fears and vulnerabilities.

"We need to talk," he said. "In private."

She looked at him, and then looked away. "Now? I don't see that there is any way they are coming. I was just asking about the chances of getting some flight schedules changed."

Despite the fact she *knew* Allie and Joe weren't coming, despite the fact that she had asked Tandu about canceling, despite the fact that she was trying to figure out how to get rid of all these people, he saw it, just for a second, wink behind her bright eyes.

Hope.

Against all odds, his beautiful, funny, bookish, spunky Becky was still hoping for a happy ending.

"We need to talk," Drew told her.

She hesitated, scanned the sky for an incoming jet and then sighed. "Yes, all right," she said.

He led her away from the crowded front lawn and front terrace.

"I just talked to Joe," he said in a low voice.

"And? Is everything okay? Between you?"

This was who she really was: despite it all, despite thinking that he had betrayed her trust, she was worried about him and his troubled relationship with his brother, first. And the wedding second.

"I guess time will tell."

"You didn't patch things up," she said sadly.

"He didn't phone to patch things up. Becky, he gave me some bad news."

"Is he all right?" There it was again, a boundless compassion for others. "What?" she whispered.

"There isn't going to be a wedding."

It was then that he knew she had been holding her breath, waiting for a miracle, because the air whooshed out of her and her shoulders sagged.

"Because of the press finding out?" she said.

"No, Becky, there was never going to be a wedding."

She looked at him with disbelief.

"Apparently this whole thing—" he swept his arm to indicate the whole thing "—was just a giant ruse planned out in every detail by Allie. She sent the press here, yesterday morning, on a wild-goose chase."

"It wasn't you," she whispered. Her skin turned so pale he wondered if she was going to faint.

"Of course it wasn't me."

She began to tremble. "But how are you ever going to forgive me for thinking it was you?"

"I don't believe," he said softly, "that you ever did believe that. Not in your heart."

"Why did she do that?" Becky wailed.

"So that she and my brother could sneak away and get married in peace. Which they did. An hour ago. In Topeka, Kansas, of all places."

Her hand was on his arm. She was looking at him searchingly. "Your brother got married without you?"

He lifted a shoulder.

"Oh! That is absolutely unforgivable!"

"It's not your problem."

"Oh, my God! Here I am saying what is unforgivable in other people, and what I did was unforgivable. I accused you of alerting the press!"

"Is it possible," he asked her softly, "that you wanted to be mad at me? Is it possible it was just one last-ditch effort to protect yourself from falling in love with me?"

She was doing now what she had not done when he told her there would be no wedding. She was crying.

"I'm so sorry," she said.

"Is it true then? Are you in love with me?"

"Yes, I'm afraid it is. It's true."

"It's true for me, too. I'm in love with you, Becky. I am so in love with you. And I'm as terrified as you are. I'm afraid of loving. I'm afraid of loss. I'm afraid I can't be the man you need me to be. I'm afraid…"

She stopped him with her lips. She stopped him by twining her hands around his neck and pulling him close to her.

And when she did that, he wasn't afraid of anything anymore.

CHAPTER SEVENTEEN

"WHY DID SHE do all this?" Becky asked.

"Joe told me that she never told any of these people they were coming to a wedding."

"She didn't! That's true. She told them in appreciation for their kindness they were being invited to a celebration of love. I saw some of the invitations today. It doesn't really answer *why* she did all this, does it? All this tremendous expense for a ruse? There are a million things that would have been easier and cheaper to send the press in the wrong direction so they could get married in private."

"Joe told me why she did it."

"And?"

"Joe told me that people would look at her humble beginnings and share personal stories about themselves. And so she sent invitations to the ones with the most compelling personal stories, a comeback from cancer, a bankruptcy, surviving the death of a child.

"Joe says she has thought of nothing else for months—that she did her homework. That she chose the ones who rose above their personal circumstances and still gave back to others.

"He said those are the ones they want to celebrate love with them. He said Allie wants her story to bring hope to lives where too many bad things had occurred. He says she's determined to make miracles happen."

"Wow," Becky said softly. "It almost makes me not want to be mad at her."

"Regretfully, me, too."

They laughed softly together.

"It's quite beautiful, isn't it?" Becky said quietly.

He wanted to harrumph it. He wanted to say it was impossibly naive and downright dumb. He wanted to say his future sister-in-law—no, make that his current sister-in-law—was showing signs of being extraordinarily clever about manipulating others.

He wanted to say all that, but somehow he couldn't.

Because here he was, the beneficiary of one of the miracles that Allie Ambrosia had been so determined to make happen.

You heal now, Tandu had said to him. And somehow his poor wounded heart had healed, just enough to let this woman beside him past his defenses. Now, he found himself hoping they would have the rest of their lives to heal each other, to get better and better.

"You know, Becky, all those people are expecting a wedding. Tandu said it's impossible to put a hold on the food now."

"It's harder to reschedule those exit flights than you might think."

"The minister is already here. And so is the photographer."

"What of it?"

"I think any wedding that is a true expression of love will honor why we are all here."

"What are you suggesting?"

"I don't think she ever had that dress made to hurt you."

"Oh, my God." Becky's fist flew to her mouth, and tears shone behind her eyes.

"And I've been thinking about this. There is no way my brother would ever get married without me. Not unless he thought it was for my own good."

"They put us together deliberately!"

"I'm afraid that's what I'm thinking."

"It's maddening."

"Yes."

"It's a terrible manipulation."

"Yes."

"It's like a blind date on steroids."

"Yes."

"Are you angry?"

"No."

"Me, neither."

"Because it worked. If they would have just introduced us over dinner somewhere, it would have never worked out like this."

"I know. You would have seen me as a girl from Moose Run, one breath away from becoming a nun."

"You would have seen me as superficial and arrogant and easily bored."

"You would have never given me a second chance."

"You wouldn't have wanted one."

They were silent for a long time, contemplating how things could have gone, and how they did.

"What time is the wedding?" he asked her.

"It's supposed to be at three."

"That means you have one hour and fifteen minutes to make up your mind."

"I've made up my mind," Becky whispered.

"You should put on that dress and we should go to that gazebo I built, and in the incredible energy of two hundred people who have been hand-chosen for the bigness of their hearts, we should get married."

"It won't be real," she whispered. "I mean, not legal. It will be like we're playing roles."

"Well, I won't be playing a role, and I don't think you're capable of it. We'll go to Kansas when it's all over. In three days we'll have a license."

"Are you asking me to marry you? For real? Not as part of Allie's amazing pretend world?"

"Absolutely, 100 percent for real."

She stared at him. She began to laugh, and then cry. She threw her arms around his neck. "Yes! Yes! Yes!" she said.

All the helicopters had gone away. The world was perfect and silent and sacred.

Despite the fact they were using up a great deal of that one hour and fifteen minutes, they talked. They talked about children. And where they would live. And what they would do. They talked about how Tandu seemed as if he was a bit of a matchmaker, too, leaving Drew to doctor Becky's leg when he had been more than capable of doing it himself, of delivering them to the best and most romantic places on the island, of "seeing" the future.

Finally, as the clock ticked down, they parted ways with a kiss.

Tandu was waiting for her when she arrived back at the castle. He took in her radiant face with satisfaction.

"You need my help to be best bride ever?"

"How do you know these things?" she asked him.

"I see."

"I know you're a medical student at Oxford."

He chuckled happily. "That is when *seeing* is the most helpful."

Tandu accompanied her up the stairs, but when she went to go to her room, Tandu nudged her in a different direction. "Take the bridal suite."

Becky stared at him suspiciously. "Have you been in on this all along?"

He smiled. "Allie has been to Sainte Simone before. I count her as my friend. I will go let the guests know there has been a slight change in plan and arrange some helpers. I will look after everything."

She could not argue with him. All her life she had never been able to accept good things happening to her, but she was willing to change. She was willing to embrace each gift as it was delivered.

Had she not been delivered a husband out of a storybook? Why not believe? She went to the bridal suite, and stood before the dress that she had hung up days before. She touched it, and it felt not unlike she had been a princess sleeping, who was now waking up.

Tandu had assembled some lovely women helpers and she was treated like a princess. Given that the time until the wedding was so brief, Becky was pampered shamelessly. Her hair was done, her makeup was applied.

And then the beautiful dress was delivered to her. She closed her eyes. Becky let her old self drop away with each stich of her clothing. The dress, and every dream that had been sewn right into the incredible fabric, skimmed over her naked skin. She heard the zipper whisper up.

"Look now," one of her shy helpers instructed.

Becky opened her eyes. Her mouth fell open. The most beautiful princess stood in front of her, her hair piled up on top of her head, with little tendrils kissing the sides of her face. Her eyes, expertly made-up, looked wide and gorgeous. Her cheekbones looked unbelievable. Her lips, pink glossed and slightly turned up in an almost secretive smile, looked sensual.

Her eyes strayed down the elegant curve of her neck to the full enchantment of the dress.

The vision in the mirror wobbled like a mirage as her eyes filled with tears.

The dress was a confection, with its sweet-heart neckline and fitted bodice, and layers and layers and layers of filmy fabric flowing out in that full skirt with an impossible train. It made her waist look as if a man could span it with his two hands.

Shoes were brought to her, and they looked, fantastically, like the glass slippers in fairy tales.

All those years ago this dress had been the epitome of her every romantic notion. Becky had been able to picture herself in it, but she had never been able to picture it being Jerry that she walked toward.

Because she had never felt like she felt in this moment.

She was so aware that the bride's beauty was not created by the dress. The dress only accen-tuated what was going on inside, that bubbling fountain of life that love had built within her.

"No crying! You'll ruin your makeup."

But everyone else in the room was crying, all of them feeling the absolute sanctity of this moment, when someone who has been a girl realizes she is ready to be a woman. When someone who has never known the reality of love steps fully into its light.

A beautiful bouquet of island flowers was placed in her hands.

"This way."

Still in a dream, she moved down the castle stairs and out the door. The grounds that had been such a beehive of activity were strangely deserted. A golf cart waited for her and it whisked her silently down the wide path, through the lushness of the tropical growth, to the beach.

She walked down that narrow green-shaded trail to where it opened at the beach. The chairs were all full. If anyone was disappointed that it was not Allie who appeared at the edge of the jungle, it did not show on a single face.

If she had to choose one word to explain the spirit she walked in and toward it would be *joy*.

Bart Lung bowed to her and offered her his arm. She kicked off the glass slippers and felt her feet sink into the sand. She was so aware that she felt as if she could feel every single grain squish up between her toes.

A four-piece ensemble began to play the traditional wedding march.

She dared to look at the gazebo. If this weren't true, this was the part where she would wake up. In her nightmares the gazebo would be empty.

But it was not empty. The minister that she had welcomed on the first plane stood there in purple cleric's robes, beaming at her.

And then Drew turned around.

Becky's breath caught in her throat. She faltered, but the light that burned in his eyes picked her up and made her strong. She moved across the space between them unerringly, her eyes never leaving his, her sense of wonder making it hard to breathe.

She was marrying this man. She was marrying this strong, funny, thrillingly handsome man who would protect those he loved with his life. She was the luckiest woman in the world and she knew it.

Bart let go of her arm at the bottom of the stairs, and Becky went to Drew like an arrow aimed straight for his heart.

She went to him like someone who had been lost in the wilderness catching sight of the way home.

She went to him with his children already being born inside her.

She repeated the vows, those age-old vows, feeling as if each word had a deep meaning she had missed before.

And then came these words:

"I now pronounce you husband and wife."

And before the minister could say anything more, Becky turned and cast her beautiful bouquet at the gathering and went into his arms and claimed his lips.

And then he picked her up and carried her down the steps and out into the ocean, and with the crowd cheering madly, he kissed her again, before he wrapped his arms tightly around her and they both collapsed into the embrace of a turquoise sea.

When they came up for air, they were laughing and sputtering, her perfect hair was ruined, her makeup was running down her face and her dress was clinging to her in wet ribbons.

"This has been the best day of my entire life," she told him. "There will never be another day as good as this one."

And Drew said to her, "No, that's not quite right. This day is just the beginning of the best days of our lives."

And he kissed her again, and the crowd went wild, but her world felt like a grotto of silence and peace, a place cut out of a busy world, just for them. A place created by love.

EPILOGUE

"WHO AGREED to this insanity?" Drew demanded of his wife.

"You did," Becky told him. She handed him a crying baby and scooped the other one out of the car seat that had been deposited on their living room floor.

Drew frowned at the baby and held it at arm's length. "Does he stink?"

"Probably. I don't think that's he. I think it's she. Pink ribbon in hair."

Drew squinted at the pink ribbon. It would not be beyond his brother to put the ribbon in Sam's hair instead of Sally's.

"I've changed my mind," Drew declared over the howling of the smelly baby. "I am not ready for this. I am not even close to being ready for this."

"Well, it's too late. Your brother and Allie are gone to Sainte Simone. They never had a honeymoon, and if ever a couple needed one, they do."

"I'm not responsible for their choices," he groused, but he was aware it was good-naturedly. His sister-in-law, Allie, was exasperating. And flaky. She was completely out of touch with reality, and her career choice of pretending to be other people had made that quality even more aggravating in her. She believed, with a childlike enthusiasm, in the fairy tales she acted out, and was a huge proponent of happily-ever-after.

And yet…and yet, could you ask for anyone more genuinely good-hearted than her? Or generous? Or kind? Or devoted to her family in general, and his brother in particular?

There was no arguing that Joe, his sweet, shy brother, had blossomed into a confident and happy man under the influence of his choice of a life partner.

In that Hollywood world where a marriage could be gone up in smoke in weeks, Allie and Joe seemed imminently solid. They had found what they both longed for most: that place called home. And they were not throwing it away.

"Mommy gone? Daddy gone?"

Drew juggled the baby, and stared down at

one more little face looking up at him. It occurred to him now would be a bad time to let his panic show.

"Yes, Andrew," he said quietly, "You're staying with Uncle Drew and Aunt Becky for a few days."

"Don't want to," Andrew announced.

That makes two of us.

Joe and Allie had adopted Andrew from an orphanage in Brazil not six months after they had married. The fact that the little boy was missing a leg only seemed to make them love him more. He'd only been home with them for about a month when they had found out they were pregnant. The fact that they had been pregnant with twins had been a surprise until just a few weeks before Sam and Sally had been born.

But the young couple had handled it with aplomb.

Drew could see what he had never seen before: that Joe longed for that sense of family they had both lost even more than he himself had. Joe had chosen Allie, out of some instinct that Drew did not completely understand, as the woman who could give him what he longed for.

So, Joe and Allie were celebrating their second anniversary with a honeymoon away from their three children.

And Drew and Becky would celebrate their second anniversary, one day behind Joe and Allie, with a pack of children, because Allie had announced they were the only people she would trust with her precious offspring.

"I wish I had considered the smell when I agreed to this," he said. "How are we going to have a romantic anniversary now?"

"Ah, we'll think of something," Becky said with that little wink of hers that could turn his blood to liquid lava. "They have to sleep sometime."

"Are you sure?"

"It will be good practice for us," she said. She said it very casually. Too casually. She shot him a look over the tousled dandelion-fluff hair of the baby she was holding.

He went very still. He moved the baby from the crook of one arm to the crook of the other. He stared at his wife, and took in the radiant smile on her face as she looked away from him and gazed at the baby in her arms.

"Good practice for us?"

Andrew punched him in the leg. "I hate you," he decided. "Where's my daddy?"

Becky threw back her head and laughed.

And he saw it then. He wondered how he had missed it, he who thought he knew every single nuance of his wife's looks and personality and moods.

He saw that she was different. Becky was absolutely glowing, softly and beautifully radiant.

"Yes," she said softly. "Good practice for us."

Andrew kicked him again. Drew looked down at him. Soon, sooner than he could ever have prepared for, he was going to have a little boy like this. A boy who would miss him terribly when he went somewhere. Who would look to him for guidance and direction. Who would think he got up early in the morning and put out the sun for him.

Or maybe he would have a little girl like the one in his arms, howling and stinky, and so, so precious it could steal a man's breath away. A little girl who would need him to show her how to throw a baseball so that the boys wouldn't make her think less of herself. And who would one day, God forbid, need him to sort through all the boys who wanted to date her to find one that might be suitable.

How could a man be ready for that?

He looked again into his wife's face. She

was watching him with a soft, knowing smile playing across the fullness of her lips.

That's how he could be ready.

Because love made a man what he could never hope to be on his own. Once, because of the loss of those he had loved the most, he'd thought it was the force that could take a man's strength completely.

Now he saw that all love wove itself into the person a man eventually became. His parents were with him. Becky's love shaped him every day.

And made him ready for whatever was going to happen next.

Andrew punched him again. Juggling the baby, he bent down and scooped Andrew up in his other arm.

"I know," he said. "I know you miss your daddy."

Andrew wailed his assent and buried his head in Drew's neck. The stinky baby started to cry. Becky laughed again. He leaned over and kissed her nose.

And it felt as if in a life full of perfect moments, none had been more perfect than this one.

Daddy. He was going to be a daddy.

It was just as he had said to her the day they

had gotten married. It wasn't the best day of their lives. All that was best was still in front of him, in a future that shone bright in the light of love. That love flowed over him from the look in her eyes. It flowed over him and drenched him and all of those days that were yet to come in its shimmering light.

* * * * *

LARGER-PRINT BOOKS!
GET 2 FREE LARGER-PRINT NOVELS PLUS
2 FREE GIFTS!

♥HARLEQUIN®

Romance

From the Heart, For the Heart

YES! Please send me 2 FREE LARGER-PRINT Harlequin® Romance novels and my 2 FREE gifts (gifts are worth about $10). After receiving them, if I don't wish to receive any more books, I can return the shipping statement marked "cancel." If I don't cancel, I will receive 4 brand-new novels every month and be billed just $5.09 per book in the U.S. or $5.49 per book in Canada. That's a savings of at least 15% off the cover price! It's quite a bargain! Shipping and handling is just 50¢ per book in the U.S. and 75¢ per book in Canada.* I understand that accepting the 2 free books and gifts places me under no obligation to buy anything. I can always return a shipment and cancel at any time. Even if I never buy another book, the two free books and gifts are mine to keep forever.

119/319 HDN GHWC

Name _____ (PLEASE PRINT)

Address _____ Apt. #

City _____ State/Prov. _____ Zip/Postal Code

Signature (if under 18, a parent or guardian must sign)

Mail to the **Reader Service:**
IN U.S.A.: P.O. Box 1867, Buffalo, NY 14240-1867
IN CANADA: P.O. Box 609, Fort Erie, Ontario L2A 5X3

Want to try two free books from another line?
Call 1-800-873-8635 or visit www.ReaderService.com.

* Terms and prices subject to change without notice. Prices do not include applicable taxes. Sales tax applicable in N.Y. Canadian residents will be charged applicable taxes. Offer not valid in Quebec. This offer is limited to one order per household. Not valid for current subscribers to Harlequin Romance Larger-Print books. All orders subject to credit approval. Credit or debit balances in a customer's account(s) may be offset by any other outstanding balance owed by or to the customer. Please allow 4 to 6 weeks for delivery. Offer available while quantities last.

Your Privacy—The Reader Service is committed to protecting your privacy. Our Privacy Policy is available online at www.ReaderService.com or upon request from the Reader Service.

We make a portion of our mailing list available to reputable third parties that offer products we believe may interest you. If you prefer that we not exchange your name with third parties, or if you wish to clarify or modify your communication preferences, please visit us at www.ReaderService.com/consumerchoice or write to us at Reader Service Preference Service, P.O. Box 9062, Buffalo, NY 14240-9062. Include your complete name and address.

HRLP15

"It's not a race, Maddison. Slow down and smell the roses—or at least enjoy the view."

"Slowing down is for losers. You'd be eaten alive in Manhattan," she threw back. "No! Darn it! Ugh. I'm trapped in a swamp! Kit! Stop laughing…"

He came up beside her, slow and easy, folding his arms and eyes dancing with amusement as he took her in. "Pride comes before a fall."

"I haven't fallen." Maddison tried to summon some shred of dignity, hard as it was to do when one foot was caught fast in a mini swamp, the other scrabbling for a firm foothold. Any minute now she was going to tumble and she'd be damned if she was going to fall in front of this man. Any man.

"Yet," Kit pointed out helpfully.

"You could help me."

"I could." The laughter underpinned his words and she glared at him.

"Do you want me to beg?"

"Well…" He leaned in close and her breath hitched.

His face was barely centimeters from hers, his shoulder close enough to grab, to hold on to, to bury herself in and let herself be saved.

She didn't need saving, did she? Just a helping hand.

"You could say *please*."

Their eyes caught, held. His were alive with laughter, a teasing warmth curving his mouth, but behind the amusement was something hotter, something deeper, something straining to break through. And Maddison knew, with utter certainty, that all she needed to do was ask.

She glared, watching his amusement increase until a reluctant smile curved her lips. "Please."

"There, that wasn't so hard, was it?" Kit grasped her hand and pulled. "Easy, Maddison, I got you."

He had. His arms were around her, steadying her, holding her up, and she allowed herself to be held, to be steadied. Just for a second. What harm could it do? One moment of needing someone else? Just a moment and then she would pull back, make some quip and carry on, because that was what Maddison Carter did, right? She carried on.

"Thanks." Her breath was short, and as she looked into his eyes, any urge to laugh the moment off fell away. All the amusement had drained out of his face, out of those blue eyes, now impossibly molten like sapphire forged in some great furnace. Instead she looked into the sharp planes of his face and saw want. She saw need. She saw desire.

For her.

Don't miss
IN THE BOSS'S CASTLE by Jessica Gilmore,
available May 2016 wherever
Harlequin® Romance books and ebooks are sold.

www.Harlequin.com

HREXP0416R